W9-DHU-217

Murder at Hampton Court Palace

Murder at Hampton Court Palace

Teresa Collard

This first world edition published in Great Britain 1992 by
SEVERN HOUSE PUBLISHERS LTD of
35 Manor Road, Wallington, Surrey SM6 0BW
First published in the U.S.A. 1992 by
SEVERN HOUSE PUBLISHERS INC of
475 Fifth Avenue, New York, NY 10017–6220.

British Library Cataloguing in Publication Data
Collard, Teresa
Murder at hampton court palace.
I. Title
823.914 [F]

ISBN 0-7278-4343-5

Typeset by Hewer Text Composition Services, Edinburgh
Printed and bound in Great Britain by Billing and Sons Ltd, Worcester

For my husband Ken Brierley

Acknowledgments

I wish to acknowledge the assistance given me by Dr Michael Bullivant, Michael de la Pena, Dr Jane Pilgrim, Hilary Davan Wetton, Crawford Macdonald, Administrator of Hampton Court Palace, and Glyn George, Operations Manager who, because he is a mine of information, has steered me clear of many pitfalls.

1

Why, wondered Professor Lawrence Berkeley, had he ever agreed to act as cicerone to the New Jersey Tudor Society? He should have realised that the members were all dead set on getting their money's worth; Warwick Castle, Broughton Castle, Blenheim, Stratford-upon-Avon, Upton House, Charlecote, Sulgrave Manor, and finally Hampton Court Palace, all in one week. Hampton Court contained treasures enough for ten palaces, its walls oozed history, every stone told a story, its gardens too. How could he, in four hours, do justice to the place? Thank God this was the penultimate day. Tomorrow, he thought, I'll be shot of them. They'll be winging their way back to Kennedy leaving me in peace. No more aggro, no more tension, no more complaints about swollen feet, or the lack of leg room, or the unfairness of bloody-minded people who always grab the front seats. Worse than dealing with children, thought the Professor, as those who claimed lineage back to Tudor England streamed out of the Randolph Hotel in Oxford and clambered on to the coach.

At the same moment as the coach left the Randolph, Jane Stormont, living in Hanwell-on-the-Hill, only twenty-five miles north of Oxford, was gazing at a car she'd never seen in the village before. For the third time the driver of the white Cavalier hatchback drove past the Old Rectory. He appeared to be more interested in the entrance to the Rectory than in the fifteenth-century church with its unusual lychgate. Peering at him from behind her desk in the spare room, which she now used as an office, Jane felt vaguely uneasy. Damn! She'd lost the thread. Wrestling with her translation of Ibsen's *An Enemy of the People* was difficult enough without added distractions. She tried once again to concentrate on Dr Stockman, a fighter for freedom and truth who held a theory that the majority was never right, but it was no good. She gave up. All she could think about was the stranger, dark skinned, possibly an Arab; but what would an Arab want in a small village like Hanwell-on-the-Hill? If he was lost why didn't he call at the village post office? Win or Roger would soon put him right. Was she being stupid? Was she over-reacting, she wondered? Was she dreaming up a scenario too far-fetched for words? Words she'd never utter to Peter, not after last time, when he'd laughed at her and played down the incident. Told her she was frightening the children. Nothing she might say could be more frightening than their experience in the woods, abutting the castle, when they were out walking with their father. Two shots were fired in their direction. Pete threw himself to the ground dragging Sandra and Stephen down with him. One shot whistled past his ear embedding itself in a tree, and the other went straight through the crown of his ridiculous hat. Fortunately the bullet was at the end of its trajectory and unstable otherwise Pete would have ended up as cold meat in the mortuary. He'd laughed it off. 'An inexperienced poacher,' was all he'd say. Nobody, thought Jane, shoots pheasant in May, not even poachers.

She gave up on Dr Stockman and went down to the kitchen to make a cup of coffee. She stopped on the landing halfway down the stairs, and looked through the small stained-glass window at the church. It was a view she loved. The colours in the window together with the brilliance of the sun produced a strange effect making the grey Celtic cross on the right of the church look pink. The yews too assumed a curious texture, but even more curious was the figure standing motionless near the west door, well camouflaged amid a deep shadow thrown by a yew tree. She half closed her eyes trying, despite the glaring sun, to form a clearer picture. It was the same man, no mistake about it. It was the same man now looking in her direction, with no interest whatsoever in the church. She didn't think twice. She ran downstairs and picked up the phone. She'd speak to Peter. He wouldn't like being interrupted, he never did.

Lady Stormont answered the phone. 'You sound worried, Jane. What is it?'

'Nothing, Mother . . . I just wanted to know . . . to know whether Pete's expecting a visitor here today . . . here in Hanwell?'

'Got his dates mixed up again, has he? Hang on, my dear, I'll tell him to pick up the extension.'

Pamela Stormont hurried out of her sitting-room, and down the corridor to a small study which she'd placed at her son's disposal.

'What is it, Mother?' he asked automatically as he went on with his preparation for a twelve o'clock meeting with the Minister of Defence.

'It's Jane on the phone. She sounds worried.'

'Damn. She knows how I hate being disturbed during the day, especially with things coming to a head.'

His mother wondered what things, but both she and her daughter-in-law had the good sense not to question Peter about his work.

'It's something to do with a visitor in Hanwell.'

'What! Oh, in that case I'll have a quick word.' He lifted the phone.

Lady Stormont closed the door quietly and returned to her sitting-room. She stood in her grace and favour apartment at Hampton Court Palace gazing at the vast sweeping lawn wondering how Peter with his diabetes managed to get up at five o'clock every morning, work through until eight o'clock, stop briefly for a cup of tea and a piece of toast and then settle down again and work until lunchtime. It was not surprising that with such ceaseless energy and application he'd managed a double first at Cambridge, and since his graduation fifteen years ago had gone from strength to strength. He owed a great deal of his success to Paul Burgess who'd been his professor and mentor at Cambridge, a man who made sure his star pupil met all the right people. The two men became close friends and Paul who was married, but with no progeny, became godfather to Pete's twins, but when he gave up his chair at Cambridge to become chairman of a national oil company, they'd gone their own ways.

Peter waited until he heard the phone being replaced before speaking. 'What is it, Jane?' he asked brusquely.

'Sorry to disturb you, darling, but there's a man hanging about outside who appears to be interested in the house.'

'So?'

'He's prowling about in the churchyard at the moment.'

'That's what people do, Jane. They prowl around in churchyards looking at tombstones, reading epitaphs.'

'He's not interested in the damned tombstones. He's only interested in our house.'

'Why not! A fine example of Georgian architecture. Of course people stand and stare.'

'That's not all,' said Jane, distinctly uptight. 'He drove past the house three times this morning taking a good look at the entrance. I am almost certain he's an Arab.'

'Aren't you imagining things? Probably as English as I am, but I've too much work on hand to bother about acquiring a suntan.'

'Peter, you're impossible.'

'Jane, darling, please calm down. I'll be back tomorrow and we'll talk about it then.'

'What time will you be home?'

'In time to take the band rehearsal at seven o'clock so

don't bother to cook for me. A sandwich will do.'

'Mac told you to be careful with your diet. Cut out the bread and eat more protein.'

'Ah, that reminds me. I need more pills, get him to give you a prescription.'

'I have done, they're in the bathroom.'

'Thanks, Jane, where would I be without you? Now I must get on. I have a lunchtime meeting with Hubert Morrissey.'

Peter replaced the phone and sighed. For the last few weeks Jane and the children had been much safer with him out of the way, but he couldn't go into all that. He hated not being with them, but while working so closely with the Ministry of Defence, spending three days a weeks with his mother at Hampton Court solved all the logistics, near enough to London to be there in half an hour, and by train which was an added bonus. Well tucked away; only his secretary and the Minister knew where to reach him. Discussions took place either in the apartment or on fine days strolling round the gardens, and on top of all that his mother laid on an excellent lunch. It meant also that present developments on the project in hand were kept inviolate in his mother's safe. Nothing on the laboratory computer for snoopers to pick up. Too much research had been filched that way. All the data, thank the Lord, would be handed over to Morrissey after lunch, then he could continue with his own experiments, which if successful, would radically improve the environment. His eyes wandered to the photograph taken by his mother during the Easter holidays, but like all her efforts at photography it was slightly out of focus. Nine-year-old Stephen could do better with his Kodak. Jane looked beautiful with her shoulder-length auburn hair caught in the breeze, her arms round the twins, both blond enough to be mistaken for Swedes. Jane was putting on a bit of weight, no longer disporting a sylph-like figure. It suited her, but why did she always have to hide her lovely long legs under calf-length skirts? At thirty-three she could easily be taken for twenty-five, but he looked forty-eight, not thirty-eight. His receding hairline was flecked with grey, and he was lean with the physique of an athlete, which owed nothing to prolonged exercise. Occasional walks with the children, waving his arms in the air once a week at band practice, and running up and down the stairs at the lab kept his figure in trim. He sighed again. He'd be glad when the present project was through and he could return home, and continue with the work he'd initiated nearly two years ago at Oxford. Only his closest colleagues were totally in the picture, really understood the extent to which the invention could be used. Many inventors had come up with prototypes, all too expensive to run, but he'd virtually solved that problem, and the initial cost could be kept down to reasonable proportions.

Hubert Morrissey, Minister for Defence, arrived early. If only, he thought, he had enough time in the world he would have travelled by river boat, but the PM had called him for a three p.m. meeting at Number Ten, and no one was ever late for that. As Simmons, his chauffeur, brought the Rolls to a standstill he called Peter on his car phone.

'Dr Stormont,' said the Minister, who never wasted time on superfluous introductions, 'do you know something, I've never seen the interior of the palace. Why don't we converse for an hour as we walk round the place, have lunch as planned and then firm up on our discussions after lunch?'

'Suits me, Minister. Great Gatehouse in five minutes' time, say 11.50?'

'Splendid,' responded the Minister. 'I'll be there.'

Simmons, who'd listened to the conversation, smiled to himself, and waited for the Minister to say what he'd expected to hear.

'Simmons, didn't you say that as a lad you'd often visited Hampton Court?'

'Yes, sir.'

'Then you can direct me to the Great Gatehouse?'

'Yes, sir. Follow me.'

Hubert Morrissey had been in politics a long time, but not one teacher at his grammar school would have given him a snowball's chance in hell of making a name for himself. A small grey man, an easily forgettable man, but a great infiltrator. Always at the side of those making decisions. Always ready to step into the breach. A valued aide, a good second in command who eventually became a parliamentary private secretary. But he wanted more, and when the lady bowled her ninepins down one by one he was around and her eyes lighted upon him. *Rise, Sir Walter*, said fellow members behind his back. The latterday Raleigh gazed, with apparent interest, at a coat of arms carved over the doorway but his mind dwelt on Lady Stormont's kitchen, wondering what delicacy she was preparing this time.

'Stunning,' said Sir Hubert, as Peter Stormont arrived. 'What an imposing entrance.'

'It nearly collapsed in the eighteenth century. The top two floors, I believe, were removed and the whole structure rebuilt. But wait until you see the Great Hall.'

The Minister followed his host up a flight of stone steps once trodden by the Tudors as they gathered to be royally entertained with a sumptuous banquet, or a masquerade and revels continuing until the early hours.

'My God, it's imposing,' said Morrissey as they entered, 'truly majestic.'

'Would you care to hire an audio cassette?' asked an attendant standing in shadow at the entrance to the hall.

'No thanks, not today,' said Sir Hubert. 'I'm lucky enough to have a guide with me.'

Not everyone was so lucky. The young woman following

them decided she couldn't do without such instant painless instruction. Once the headphones were in place she made for the vast flagstone in the centre of the Great Hall which marked the site of an ancient open hearth. She stood immobile for some minutes, gazing up in obvious wonder at the huge hammer-beam roof. Hubert Morrissey was more interested in the windows.

'Look at that stained glass, Dr Stormont. Henry VIII, standing with his feet wide apart to support that massive frame of his; solid, immovable. Presumably those heraldic shields topped by crowns are the arms of his six unfortunate queens?'

'Not all unfortunate,' murmured Peter.

'Oh, I think they were. Any woman who became embroiled with Henry paid the price in one way or another. Two beheaded, two sent packing, one died in childbirth, and the last, a lady who knew full well there were schemes afoot to unseat her, kept her head, only because she kept her head.'

Peter laughed. 'Sounds like modern-day politics.'

'Yes, human nature doesn't change.'

As Simmons wandered back to the Rolls he saw a party of Americans making their way towards the Great Gatehouse. He watched with some amusement as the tall guy with grey hair, who appeared to be the guide, tried to deal with a barrage of questions. Finally the leader gave up, raised his hand, and walked purposefully towards the main entrance.

Professor Lawrence Berkeley decided to take his time, let them rush ahead, swoon when they saw the Great Hall, scream with delight when they recognised any reference to the Tudors, work out for themselves the armorial bearings, and rave about the costumes depicted in the portraits which they were all going to copy for their Tudor Ball on October 1st.

* * *

By the time the Minister and Dr Stormont reached the Queen's State Apartments they were totally engrossed in discussing methods of defence. They spoke softly, but if anyone heard the odd sentence of their quietly spoken dialogue it would, out of context, prove to be totally meaningless. They stopped for some time in the Queen's Drawing Room apparently gazing at the multitudes milling around the gardens enjoying the fountain, and the Long Water flanked each side by an avenue of yew trees. They saw very little. Sir Hubert listened while his companion expanded on recent reductions in armaments. A reduction in tanks would prove to be in Britain's interests. With their new invention tanks would be immune from every type of attack other than a nuclear bomb. The smart efficient-looking blonde-haired female warder wondered why the two men moving like zombies through each room weren't showing much interest. They'd hardly looked at the pictures, furniture, furnishings, or superb decor. They were far more interested in what they were saying than what they were seeing. She heard the odd words . . . global warfare . . . ground safety . . . and freedom of movement. It's just as well, she thought, that most of our visitors are more interested in the history of this place than those two. At least the tall young woman following in their wake was not wasting her time. Overly tall for a woman, thought Doris Veasey, with a mass of dark curly hair which fell across her face hiding her features. Perhaps being tall explained why her feet were so large, but she was painfully thin, and wearing a floral hip-length blouse, in an effort to camouflage her shape? Must have been slimming. Stupid some women, why didn't they make the most of what they'd been given? She'd had the sense, though, to hire an audio cassette.

Simmons, who was a great self-educator, sat in the Rolls eating his lunch, listening to advanced French on a

Linguaphone tape. He'd been doing very well indeed. He could even converse with the Minister when Sir Hubert was feeling in the mood, the dialogue a little stilted, perhaps, but none the less understandable. Simmons felt good. Sally, as usual, had done him proud; smoked salmon sandwiches (albeit Pacific), a chocolate mousse laced with brandy followed by Bath Olivers, Stilton, and Kenyan coffee. He enjoyed his life, felt at the centre of events, kept in touch, listened, learned, and returned home at the end of the day a contented man, not like some of the lads who resented the lifestyle of their passengers, resented being at their beck and call, resented never being more than a fly on the wall. That was what Simmons enjoyed more than anything else . . . he enjoyed being that fly.

Only a few more minutes. Sir Hubert always kept good time. He'd seen the two men emerge from the Queen's Apartments at one o'clock, knew that lunch would take an hour and the final discussion about fifteen minutes. They'd be away by 2.20. The meeting with the Prime Minister was scheduled for three o'clock at Downing Street, and to date the Minister had never been late.

Thank God, thought the Professor, in less than a week I'll be happily ensconced in Cambridge having had a ball which may shatter an old enemy. For half an hour he kept pace with Doc Jackson who, thankfully, didn't open his mouth. In fact, thought Lawrence, he'd never seen the little man in such a dark mood. Their perambulations were suddenly brought to a halt just inside the Queen's Presence Chamber. Members of the New Jersey Tudor Society were all huddled together in a vast room, all gazing at a figure peacefully asleep in a luxuriously panoplied four-poster. The Professor wondered why the authorities at Hampton Court were aping Warwick Castle and using dummies to create the feeling of a lived-in house. Not necessary, the palace had enough to offer. It didn't need gimmicks.

'They certainly do things well here,' enthused Marilyn de Grey, secretary of the society. 'It's so lifelike, better than anything at Madame Tussaud's.'

'What a modern hairstyle,' murmured Virginia Carpenter whose antecedents, all craftsmen, coopers, staymakers and stonemasons had lived and worked in Ludlow. She couldn't hope to compete with members of the society, members like James Richmond, the treasurer, who'd changed his name, legally, from Smithson to Richmond. All because his Tudor ancestor was the mother of the Duke of Richmond, one of Henry VIII's many by-blows.

'Oh gee, I'd love to see her nightwear,' sighed Judy Devereaux. Without another word she stepped over the rope, meant as a deterrent, and pulled back the heavily embroidered quilt.

'Don't touch it, Judy,' said her husband sharply.

She took no notice. She never did. 'My God,' she whispered, 'she looks so real, but why isn't she in period costume? Her clothing's quite modern.'

Her hand brushed the face of the sleeping figure. How strange, she thought, she is real, she's warm! The figure didn't stir. Judy took a closer look.

'Christ, Robert!' she screamed. 'I think she's dead.'

There was pandemonium as everyone pressed forward to see the body.

'Stand back,' ordered Doc Jackson as he elbowed his way through. Being a short man he'd not been able to see the figure in the bed, but members of the Tudor Society obeyed him. They moved back, allowed him through, and stood silently awaiting his verdict. The Professor looked on in total disbelief. How could anyone, in so public a place, crawl into bed without being seen by the warders or the general public? Marilyn de Grey, his ex-colleague from Princeton, answered his unspoken thoughts.

'No one raised the alarm, Lawrence, because she truly

looks like a waxwork. Peaceful without a care in the world.'

'She certainly hasn't any cares now,' he said sharply.

Doc Jackson shook his head. 'She sure is dead, Professor, but she's still warm. Rigor mortis hasn't set in yet. Been dead no more than an hour, that would be my guess.'

'Let me get out of here,' screamed Judy Devereaux who'd never before seen a dead body. 'I didn't travel halfway across the world for horrors like this.'

Her husband, whose ancestor's head had been severed from his body by an axeman on Tower Green, propelled her into the next room.

'For heaven's sake, Judy, calm down. The sleeping and the dead are but as pictures.'

'Cut it out, Robert,' she moaned, 'you've always got an answer.'

'Not mine,' murmured the high school teacher, 'Shakespeare's.' He put his arm round her saying no more, knowing that she'd dine out on the story, embroidered no doubt, for years to come.

A warder hurriedly pushed her way towards the Professor. With her experienced eye she recognised him as the leader of this strangely quiet group of Americans who a few moments before had been creating mayhem.

'Could you please move on?' she asked. 'Other visitors would like to see this room.'

'I think,' said Lawrence firmly, 'you'd better ask them to retrace their steps while you close off this room.'

'Why on earth should I do that?' asked Mrs Spratt.

'Because,' retorted Doc Jackson before Lawrence could intervene, 'you have a dead woman in this bed. Take a look.'

The Americans made way for Mrs Spratt who gasped when she saw the body. Her face paled and her body shook as though the temperature had suddenly dropped twenty degrees.

'I don't believe it,' she whispered. 'It isn't possible. Doris was going to take me shopping, drive me to the supermarket after we'd finished our stint . . . she was . . .'

Doc Jackson and Marilyn de Grey caught her as she fainted.

'Carry her into the next room, she needs air,' ordered the doctor.

Two of the men carried out his bidding and Marilyn followed them.

The Professor, for the first time since the tour commenced, authoritatively took charge.

'Gary,' he said to the treasurer, 'get our party clear of this room. Keep moving ahead and wait for me in Fountain Court. Virginia, you go back the way we've come. Tell everyone to wait in Base Court, then find a warder. Ask him to get someone in authority here immediately. Tell him we have a doctor, also tell him that Doris, whose surname we don't know, is dead lying in a four-poster.'

Within minutes the area had been cleared, and the head of security, who'd already called an ambulance in case the woman could be resuscitated, was on the scene. Tom Abrams was shattered when he discovered a member of his staff lying dead. He gazed down on the body of Doris Veasey thinking how strangely peaceful she looked. No lines on her face, her lips slightly parted, almost a smile on them. It looked for all the world as though, during her stretch of duty, she'd tired and climbed into bed to take an afternoon nap.

'I can't understand this,' he said to the two Americans beside the bed. 'I can't believe that Mrs Veasey of all people is lying here in this centuries-old bed.'

'You're in charge, are you?' asked the Professor.

'Yes. I'm Abrams, Captain Abrams, Head of Security.'

'And you?'

'Lawrence Berkeley.'

He looked at the tall American, whose grey hair curled over his collar, feeling that he should know him.

'Berkeley . . . Lawrence Berkeley . . . your name's certainly familiar, but I can't quite place . . .'

'The Tower of London murders, two years ago, I was there at the time.'

'Ah yes. You're the American professor who helped that detective chappie . . . Byrd, wasn't that the name?'

'Yes. Detective Superintendent James Byrd.'

'Then you, sir,' he said to the shorter man, 'must be the doctor?'

'Sorry,' said the Professor. 'This is Dr Jackson.'

Captain Abrams took a closer look at the body. 'What's your diagnosis, doctor?'

'A heart attack would be my guess.'

'But she was too young . . . much too young, not yet forty.' He sighed. 'We never know, do we, what's going to hit us.'

The doctor shook his head. He saw this sort of thing every day of his life.

What a pity, thought Tom Abrams, that this American isn't practising in Britain. It would have been so straightforward. He could have signed the death certificate here and now, and Mrs Veasey's body would have been moved in a dignified way to lie in a funeral parlour to await burial. Now she has to be taken to Kingston Hospital where a local doctor will do the necessary.

'Dr Jackson, if this had happened in the States would you have signed a death certificate?'

'Yes . . . yes after further examination . . . I believe I would.'

'Doctor, I'm grateful you were here, you too, Professor, for clearing the area so swiftly. An ambulance should be on its way.'

The three men gazed down on the immobile figure of Doris Veasey. This is utterly bizarre, thought Abrams. Nothing quite like this has ever happened in the palace before.

'Isn't life bloody unpredictable,' murmured Lawrence. 'Here one moment, snuffed the next.'

Tom nodded. 'Ever since an unpleasant divorce this place has been her life. She never took time off, she was never ill.'

'Has she any children?' asked the doctor.

'No, and I'm afraid I've no idea whether her parents are alive, but Mrs Spratt should be able to tell us. They were very close.'

'Yes, we were very close,' said a quiet voice behind him. Jean Spratt, who'd recovered, stood there, sniffing slightly. 'If only Doris had told me she wasn't feeling well . . . I . . . I . . .'

At that moment they heard the strident sound of an ambulance klaxon nearing the palace, and reaching its crescendo as it turned into the gates. Then silence.

'They didn't waste much time,' said Lawrence.

Thinking times for Hubert Morrissey were the late hours immersed in a bath or on comfortable journeys after meetings. He was hardly aware of the traffic, nor bothered by the stench of exhaust fumes which never penetrated the air-conditioned Rolls. The movement was no more than a gentle reminder that he'd left on time, and as always Simmons with his unfailing magic would arrive on time. What an excellent lunch. Lady Stormont had again done them proud. He'd been trying to give up puddings, get rid of the paunch which was beginning to assume horrendous proportions, but there was no way he could forego her crême brûlée. He must remember to send her a half case of his 1982 Saint Emilion, she'd enjoy that. Cooking, inventing, creating, what a family.

Pity the old man, who'd been a Queen's Messenger, and a most talented amateur painter, had died in that appalling plane crash. But the laurels must go to Peter Stormont, a twentieth-century Leonardo who could be equally successful as an engineer, a photo-synthesist, an inventor of board games, or a musician.

He took another look at the papers on his lap, refreshed his memory, to let the Prime Minister know, in no more than five sentences, what had been achieved. It had nothing to do with their afternoon meeting, but the PM always showed an interest, liked to be informed. Peter Stormont was a wizard. Thank God he'd refused those lucrative American offers, not for himself but for his children. His offspring, he steadfastly maintained, would remain in the North Oxfordshire village where they'd been born, and be educated in England. Money couldn't buy him. What a blessing for us all, thought the Minister, but how strange that the one talent this electronic wizard lacked was the ability to draw. The tank on the piece of paper before him looked like a shoe box with tracks, but it served its purpose. Tank protection had been tackled over the years in many ways – electronic warning of hostile radar emissions, laser warning receivers, ceramic and reactive armour, screens to divert oncoming missiles; pulses to warn the driver of hazards ahead, and the equipment to neutralise mines – all partially successful, but this new idea was a winner. It is, he thought thankfully, now out of Stormont's hands. We can go ahead with the electronic cocoon which affords protection by emitting misinformation about the characteristics of the vehicle. Stormont preferred to call it a womb because of its protective qualities. Cocoon – womb – what did the nomenclature matter as long as it did the job? Now, at long last, Special Branch could call off the surveillance on Stormont's home and on his mother's Grace and Favour apartment. The minders had done their job. Peter, he knew, was eager to get back to his laboratory in Oxford to do his own thing, pursue another brainchild. He'd been pretty close about the new project but had intimated that the next invention would, in the long run, also benefit the tank, and transport in general. Rumour had it that he was working on a new-style fuel injector to save fuel, but whether it was a failsafe transmission or an update on the braking system, this highly talented scientist would make it work.

God, what a noise! Simmons gently brought the Rolls to a standstill. An ambulance with klaxon blaring tore down the centre of the road narrowly avoiding them. The Minister switched on the intercom.

'Not seen an accident, have you?'

'No, sir.'

'Those fellows, to my mind, take unnecessary risks.'

'Someone may be dying, sir.'

'Well it could have been us the way they were driving.'

'Yes, sir,' said Simmons, half smiling to himself.

The two ambulance men, with Ben Johnson, the head warder, leading the way, ran up the stairs along a corridor and into the State Apartments. They took the situation in at a glance, not even thinking it odd that a woman lay dead in an antique four-poster. The obvious place for a body to lie. Abrams and the Professor carefully removed the priceless quilt. Doris Veasey, who'd looked so large in life, a woman whose ebullient personality filled a room, looked so small, so frail in death. As she'd clambered into bed she'd not bothered to straighten her skirt. It was up round her waist revealing white briefs with a rose motif on one side, navy-blue stockings, the self-supportive type, and still wearing one flat-heeled navy-blue shoe. Tom Abrams looked closely at the bed coverings. Thank God, nothing had been damaged.

The ambulance men lifted her gently on to a stretcher, covering her with a blanket.

Mrs Spratt couldn't let her friend go, not just like that.

'Captain Abrams,' she whispered, 'I'd like to go with Doris. She shouldn't be alone.'

He took her hand. 'You go, my dear . . . but whatever it was, remember she's out of pain.'

Lawrence watched the slow procession making its way through the State Rooms, and couldn't help thinking of another sad procession, which had taken place 400 years before. The funeral of Jane Seymour, Henry's favourite wife, who'd died after giving birth to a son and heir. Henry was inconsolable, couldn't even bear to attend the funeral service.

'Excuse me, sir,' said Johnson, 'I'll see the ambulance men safely out, and then, I suppose, you'll want the Queen's State Apartments closed?'

'Yes, that's right. Give visitors their money back but don't explain why.'

'Their money back! Only if they ask,' said Johnson grinning to himself.

'And, Ben, not a word about her death. I don't want the blasted media hammering at the doors.'

'You think a heart attack is news?' asked Lawrence.

'Here in the palace it is. I want it kept quiet. We don't want adverse publicity. Before you can say knife there'll be articles about the palace being too much of a strain for the elderly, too many stairs, not good for the heart. There aren't, of course, there are gardens, seats, and eating places, no one has to rush. I'm saying nothing. We don't want to scare the public away.'

'You won't. If America's anything to go by it will have the opposite effect. The public's insatiably curious.'

'That's not my only problem. Our Administrator, Colonel Wishart, and his wife are on a walking holiday in the

Dales, and unreachable until seven o'clock in the evening. I need to speak to him as soon as possible.'

The Professor noticed that Dwight Jackson was on edge, kept walking up and down the room staring through the windows, and muttering to himself.

'Doc,' said Lawrence quietly, 'could you get back to your members? Make sure Judy Devereaux is OK. Tell them to take a stroll in the gardens. I'll join you in a few minutes.'

The Professor waited until the doctor was out of earshot.

'What's bothering you, Captain?'

'Her shoes, Professor. Why only one? My wife's immediate reaction when she puts her feet up on the sofa is to kick 'em off. I am sure Doris Veasey would never, wittingly, have left them on.'

'What are you saying?'

'Best left unsaid.'

'Is it? Are you perhaps asking yourself, in retrospect, why you find the circumstances odd? You accepted Doc Jackson's diagnosis, as I did. Now you're not so sure.'

'I'm imagining things, Professor.'

'Shades of the past, perhaps?'

'Perhaps!'

By the time the ambulance arrived at Casualty Dr Miller had finished his frugal lunch. He was definitely losing weight, about time too, but it wasn't easy. He liked all the wrong foods, Mars bars between meals, syllabub, peach melbas and cream doughnuts, but he was determined to win the club squash tournament, and if banting was the only way, he'd do it. He washed his hands, powdered them and slipped on a pair of rubber gloves.

The woman's facial lines had faded, the body was firm,

in good trim too, he would have expected her to have seen seventy.

He carried out the usual routine. There was something about the woman, why the smile, only slight, but was that the way she dealt with pain? Apart from Miss Dior, the perfume his wife used, there was no smell which gave him a lead. He didn't feel sure . . . didn't know . . . There were no puncture marks on her arms, she didn't look like a drug addict. Food poisoning? It could be pretty swift, but he had to admit he was lost.

'Help me turn her over, nurse.'

She weighed very little, no more than eight stone.

'What's that?' he asked as he pointed to an infinitesimal scratch on the buttock. They both peered closely. Yes, that was it. A fine hypodermic had been used to empty its lethal contents into the body of an unsuspecting woman. The dose, whatever it was, had caused instant death.

'There'll have to be an autopsy, this is out of my court, nurse.'

Tom Abrams, who'd demonstrated to the Professor that he'd an innate feeling that all was not as it seemed, was not surprised when Dr Miller rang. Mrs Veasey, it seemed, had died from the effects of an unknown poison, possibly injected into her buttock, and an immediate autopsy was necessary. Damnation, he thought, this is a different ball game. He'd hoped to keep the matter quiet but this latest development would open the floodgates to the media scavengers.

Within seconds of Dr Miller's call he was on the phone to his old friend Keith Platt, officer in charge at Twickenham HQ, who lost no time in despatching the coroner's officer to Kingston Hospital to stand by while an autopsy was carried out.

Dr Patel, the pathologist, had two bodies to dissect before dealing with Mrs Veasey, which enabled Sergeant

Head to spend three hours watching cricket, his favourite sport, while imbibing endless cups of coffee in the hospital canteen.

Chief Superintendent Platt, wisely as it turned out, decided to cut through red tape . . . it was a royal palace after all . . . a valid reason for not following usual procedures . . . he'd talk directly with the Commissioner of the Metropolitan Police. He'd take advice from the top.

In the meantime Inspector Mozart and a couple of men from Forensic were sent post haste to the palace to carry out the normal routine in such cases. Sir Elwyn Rees-Davies, Commissioner of the Met, and his wife were on the point of leaving for a week's holiday in Paris to stay with the Director of the British Council. Sir Elwyn loathed the thought of incidents in any of the royal palaces, knew only too well that the Royals kept in touch with what was happening, but knew equally well that Elaine would be furious if they deferred this Parisian holiday yet again. To be safe . . . to have everything under control . . . there was a way. He thought about the the Tower Case, yes, that was the answer. He pressed a button and asked his secretary to get Sir Charles Suckling on the line.

Detective Superintendent James Byrd, who'd taken three days' leave following a case which hadn't really stretched him, was at home in his cottage on The Green at Bletchingdon digging up early potatoes when Stephanie called him.

'It's Sir Charles Suckling on the phone.'

Now what have I done? Who have I offended this time? wondered the Superintendent.

'Byrd speaking, sir.'

'Ah, Superintendent, I gather you're enjoying well-earned leave.'

'Yes, sir.'

'The Met have a problem, or at least my friend Elwyn Rees-Davies has. There's been a death at Hampton Court, poison is suspected, probably not self-inflicted. The Commissioner wants someone with a bit of weight down there immediately . . . someone who understands the set-up. Only twenty-four hours, you understand.'

'But Twickenham has some excellent men.'

'That's true. Inspector Mozart is already at the scene.'

'But surely, sir, a death like this doesn't merit interference from outside?'

'The Administrator, Colonel Wishart, is away and Captain Abrams, the Head of Security at the palace, is holding the fort. He contacted Twickenham leaving Superintendent Platt to get men in place, but Platt very shrewdly contacted the Commissioner, and spoke with him before he left for Paris. It's a royal palace, Mr Byrd, needs someone who's had experience in a similar situation, and you, of course, came to mind. Only a day or two . . . get things sorted out. Get the whole unfortunate episode in perspective. How are you fixed?'

Stephanie stood watching him, waiting on every word. He knew she'd spent all afternoon preparing a special meal, cucumber and mint soup, stuffed Aylesbury duckling accompanied by fresh potatoes and broad beans from the garden followed by a home-made raspberry pavlova.

'Well, sir, it's my wife's birthday and we were going to celebrate it by . . . by . . . by . . .'

'Forget it,' said Stephanie as she stamped out of the kitchen.

'Would you, Superintendent, call it a moveable feast?'

Knowing that Stephanie was listening, Byrd hesitated. 'Let's say, sir, that it's a freezable feast. I'll get down to Hampton Court immediately.'

Freezable, she thought. Oh no, it's not. This is the third year running that my birthday plans have been disrupted. It's never going to happen again. Never. While her husband was hastily throwing clean underwear and a shirt into an overnight bag she left the house in a furious state. She walked up the lane to the church, and sat amid the gravestones until her anger had subsided. She and Kate would celebrate her birthday. Just the two of them. It had become an annual event.

The journey down the M40 from Oxford was uneventful until he reached the roadworks south of High Wycombe. A snarl-up, seven miles long, warned Radio Oxford. Drivers would be well advised to take alternative routes. Damn, should have phoned DHQ and enquired about conditions before leaving. In his mirror he saw a police car approaching on the hard shoulder. That was the answer. He had to be quick. Now. The driver of the police car swore as he stamped on his brakes. What was that fool, standing four-square in front of his path, doing? Sergeant McGloin leapt out of the passenger seat glaring at the bearded man dressed in expensive jeans and a brilliant-orange shirt.

'What may I ask, sir, do you think you're doing?'

'Doing, Sergeant? Successfully, thank God, stopping you.'

Without another word Byrd handed his identification to the man who he knew would, at any minute, vent his spleen. Sergeant McGloin stared at the photograph of a bearded man, and then back to the subject whose dark eyes never wavered.

'I need your help, Sergeant, I must reach Hampton Court Palace as soon as possible. On a case, of course. You lead the way and I'll follow you until the road is clear.'

'Very good, sir,' said the Sergeant automatically, knowing instinctively that this man, with or without him, would have taken the hard shoulder. Never before had he seen a superintendent going out on a job dressed, in his estimation, like a yobbo.

* * *

Tom Abrams, who was in his office when Byrd arrived, showed no surprise whatsoever at the sight of the bearded hippy who entered his office.

'You haven't wasted much time, Superintendent, but do please sit down and relax for five minutes while I put you in the picture, then we'll take a look at the Queen's Presence Chamber.'

From a thermos jug he poured out two cups of piping-hot coffee.

'Help yourself to milk and sugar, Mr Byrd. This is my lifeline – I rarely eat during the day.'

Byrd wasn't surprised. The Head of Security hadn't an ounce of fat on him. The light-grey suit couldn't hide the sheer bulk of the man. He looked in his late thirties, but was probably nearer fifty, his dark hair greying at the sides was cut too short to be fashionable, his grey piercing eyes missing nothing, his mouth too big for his face; but the presence, the personality was tremendous.

'We could have done without all this, Mr Byrd. I would do anything to turn the clock back, to see Doris Veasey doing her job which she thoroughly enjoyed. Not only that an event like this is disruptive for staff and visitors. The warders are uneasy. If it could happen to Doris Veasey it could happen to anyone. It's true to say that this death has affected our entire staff of seventy-three. I want to get them back to work. Return to normal.'

James Byrd nodded sympathetically but wished he'd get on with the matter which had disrupted his family life and driven Stephanie to use words normally outside her vocabulary.

'This present incident, Mr Byrd, is bizarre in the extreme. Doris Veasey, the woman who died, was one of our five female warders. A tough, healthy, attractive woman.'

'How old?'

'Thirty-seven, and far too young to suffer a heart attack.'

'Who said she had?'

'There was a doctor on the spot shortly after it happened who wouldn't commit himself, said she might have suffered cardiac arrest, but we now know it's poison.'

'Did he attempt resuscitation?'

'No. It was too late.'

'I'm sorry, Mr Byrd, that she was moved, but as Dr Jackson thought the death due to natural causes I gave orders for her to be taken to Kingston Hospital.'

'And her family, have they been informed?'

'No. She's divorced. No children and, according to Mrs Spratt, her elderly parents are touring somewhere on the Continent . . . France . . . Spain . . . Italy, who knows? It wasn't until the ambulance had left that I began questioning the circumstances and then it was too late.'

'What circumstances?'

'She was found dead in bed, Queen Anne's bed, specially made for the Queen, and originally used at Windsor. The bed and its exquisitely embroidered trappings are magnificent. All roped off, of course, visitors can see, not touch. Now I know, Superintendent, that Doris Veasey would never have climbed into that bed, no matter how ill she felt, neither would she have kept her shoes on, at least to be more accurate, one shoe. She hated vandalism, and heavy footwear on centuries-old silk could have done untold damage. The fact that it's not torn leads me to think that, maybe, she passed out, and someone with a bizarre sense of humour placed her in the bed.'

'Yes.'

'Have you found the other one?'

'No, not yet.'

'It strikes me, Captain Abrams, that we need the results of the autopsy pronto.'

'Sergeant Head has been waiting all afternoon, but we should get them by early evening.'

'Who found the body?'

'A number of Americans were passing through . . . they thought the figure was a waxwork, but fortunately, and this is an action I would normally deplore, one of the women, eager to see what sort of night attire ladies wore in the sixteenth century, pulled back the cover and, inadvertently, touched the face. Not cold, as she'd expected, but warm, still warm. Understandably the woman went to pieces. According to Dr Jackson Mrs Veasey had been dead for less than an hour.'

'Are the Americans still here?'

'Yes, strolling in the grounds with their guide. Someone I think you may know.'

'I don't know any Americans.'

'I think you do, Superintendent. The academic who worked with you on the Tower of London murders.'

'Ah! Professor Lawrence Berkeley.'

'Perhaps, sir,' said Byrd, impatient to get down to business, 'we could take a look at the Presence Chamber, then I'd like a word with the Professor.'

'OK, Superintendent, "stand not upon the order of your going."'

As the two men were about to leave the phone rang.

'Abrams here. What!' he shouted, closing his eyes and clenching his fists.

'Who the hell . . . dammit, she was only found at one o'clock, and it's headlines you say? My God, how did they get hold of it? Thanks, Robin. At least we're forewarned and will be prepared when the damned media arrive here in force.' He replaced the receiver, shook his head, and looked bleakly at Byrd. 'That was Colonel Kilmaster from the Tower. Banner headlines. Bloody banner headlines in the early edition of the *Evening Standard*. BODY FOUND IN BED AT HAMPTON COURT PALACE. They've even named her.

The Administrator's going to love this. Fortunately I have already spoken to the proprietor and asked him to make sure Colonel Wishart rings me the moment he steps inside the hotel.'

'Where is he?'

'Walking in the Yorkshire Dales without a care in the world, until this lot hits him. Worse than that, far worse than that will be the effect on Doris Veasey's parents. They're going to pick up an English paper tomorrow, and read about the death of their only daughter. Poor sods! But who the hell's been talking?'

Abrams didn't wait for an answer. He didn't expect an answer. 'Miss Moorcroft,' he shouted, 'have you a moment?'

Colonel Wishart's secretary, who knew by the tone of Abrams' voice there was more trouble afoot, leapt up immediately and opened the door. She stood looking at both men, saying nothing. Byrd was surprised. He'd half expected a blonde bombshell, not a slender grey-haired woman, wearing tinted blue glasses, a dark green cotton dress and flat sandals.

'Miss Moorcroft,' said Tom Abrams quietly, 'today's events are already front page news, the *Evening Standard* to be exact. Will you please contact Ben Johnson and the Royal Parks Police to make sure no one, absolutely no one, gets into the building, not even Rupert Murdoch himself.'

She nodded and closed the door.

'There's your silent woman, Mr Byrd. The most efficient, capable secretary the Colonel's ever employed. She's been with him ten years, and heaven alone knows what he'll do, what any of us will do, when she goes. Boudicca, that's what we call her, Boudicca can cope with anything. Now, let's get over there then I can leave you to get on with your job.'

2

Superintendent James Byrd sat quietly for some minutes in the Queen's Presence Chamber watching the men from Forensic getting on with the job. Not really a lot they could do. Too many people had crowded round the bed, too many hands had touched the four-poster. With extreme care they removed the pillows and quilt for examination in the laboratory and covered the bed with another priceless, immaculately embroidered bedcover which the curator had provided.

Where, wondered Byrd, was Inspector Mozart, and how would he feel about someone usurping his territory, even if only for a day or two. There was very little that either he or the Inspector could do at the scene of the crime. They'd not even found the missing shoe.

He must see the Professor and his party as soon as possible, talk more fully to Captain Abrams, as well as the warders who were on duty in the State Apartments from noon onwards, and make contact with Mozart. The Americans first, he didn't want to keep them hanging about. Bad publicity wouldn't do the palace or the police any good. Using the cordless phone the Head of Security had left with him, he called the main office. Boudicca answered immediately.

'Byrd here, Miss Moorcroft. Is Inspector Mozart with you?'

'No Superintendent, he's talking to the car park attendant, and the policemen on the gates.'

'Good. I don't suppose you've any idea where I shall find Professor Berkeley and his party?'

'According to Tom Abrams he planned to continue with his schedule which included the Renaissance Picture Gallery, the Chapel Royal, the Great Vine, and the Mantegna exhibition. After that I imagine they'll take a breather in the Garden Café. In fact, they could be there now.'

'Many thanks. How do I get there?'

'Out into the forecourt, past the barrier and the works yard, turn right into Tiltyard and follow your nose.

'Good God!' said Lawrence Berkeley who was swallowing the last mouthful of a sticky Danish pastry. 'Never expected to see you here.'

'Nasty shock, is it?'

'No,' grinned the Professor, 'quite like old times. You are, presumably, investigating the lately departed lady found supine in an ancient four-poster?'

'Yes.'

Judy Devereaux, now on her third chocolate eclair, looked at the bearded newcomer with interest. Couldn't really be a policeman in that gear, and yet there was an air of authority about him.

'I found her, you know,' she blurted out.

Byrd looked at her in surprise. This wasn't a lady suffering from shock. This was a lady stuffing herself with cream cakes who was beginning to enjoy being the centre of attention.

'I know I shouldn't have touched the bed, but she looked so lifelike . . . and I was curious to see how she was dressed.'

'Perhaps it's a pity you weren't there sooner.'

'You mean she might still have been alive?'

He nodded.

'Oh God, what a terrible thought. Something else I'll

have to live with. But Doc Jackson said she'd probably suffered a heart attack.'

'Did he? Well, we can be sure of one thing,' he said cryptically, 'her heart certainly stopped.'

Byrd glanced at Lawrence and nodded at the door. 'Perhaps we could talk before I see the doctor?'

'Why not! Let's stroll round the rose garden.'

Judy, feeling distinctly peeved at being left out, looked daggers at the Tour Guide. Who did he think he was? It was her story.

'Tell everyone to stay put, Judy,' ordered the Professor.

'They're all here,' she said, distinctly miffed, 'except Sarah and Dwight.'

'Well, see if you can find them. We leave for Heathrow in half an hour.'

'Flying?' queried Byrd.

'Tomorrow. Tonight they're staying at the Hilton and returning to the States in the morning.'

'*They* are staying. Not you?'

'That's right. Brenda and I've been over here twelve months. I'm on a three-year exchange. Have taken over the Chair of History at Cambridge from Shawcross, and I'm enjoying a most comfortable Fellowship at Trinity. Should have done it years ago.'

'Brenda staying with you?'

'No. She's at our cottage in Cropredy. We bought the one next door to her sister. I join her for weekends.'

'Cambridge! Wasn't it Shawcross who filched your research and plagiarised your notes on Francis Bacon?'

'No. That was Professor Robert Kettle.'

'I guess you won't be seeing much of him.'

'On the contrary. It's water under the bridge.'

'That's not what you were saying two years ago. You were prepared to hang, draw and quarter him. Marriage has mellowed you, Lawrence.'

'You think?'

'Yes, I do. So research is out at the moment?'

'Good Lord, no. I'm still heavily into Monmouth. Remember?'

'How could I forget!'

'Professor,' said Judy in a loud whisper as he piled his debris on to a tray, 'I don't think we'll find Sarah.'

'What do you mean?'

'We heard Doc and Sarah having one hell of a slanging match. She said she'd had enough coach travel to last a lifetime. Purgatory, she said, swore she'd take a taxi to the Hilton.'

'And has she?'

'I don't know.'

'Judy, when you've finished eating,' said the Professor, wondering if she'd ever stop, 'see if you can find Doc and ask him what's happening.'

'OK, Professor. I'll get Robert organised.'

'Who's Robert?' asked Byrd as they left the café.

'Judy's poor wretched husband.'

Dwight Jackson, unseen by fellow members of the Tudor Society, stood in the Royal Pew marvelling at the splendour and perfection of the Chapel Royal. Tudor architecture at its most sumptuous. He remembered the Professor saying the Victorians had been responsible for restoring the Chapel to its former glory, but it wasn't the glory that had drawn him to the Chapel. He thought he'd caught a glimpse of Sarah in the Haunted Gallery, but she'd evaded him again, done one of her vanishing tricks soon after Judy Devereaux had found the body, and given an unforgetable histrionic performance. There was no sign of her in the Royal Pew, never easy to pick her out in a crowd . . . they were both so short. He'd wait around, sit on the bench outside, she might emerge, but why was she behaving so badly? Much worse than usual. Her menopause was playing havoc with both their lives. If only, after a busy day taking an exhausting surgery and visiting patients, he could return home and relax for an hour or two. He sighed. It hadn't been possible for months and months. When would it end?

There was so much activity . . . people in and out, and a strange lady, not looking where she was going, bumping into a young man in a tearing hurry. No, Sarah, perhaps he'd been mistaken? After waiting another fifteen minutes he slowly rose to his feet and decided to try the maze. It was the sort of place she'd choose, knowing he'd be going out of his mind looking for her.

The early roses were at their best in June, their perfume highly intoxicating.

'It's all rather splendid,' said Byrd.

'Even more splendid four centuries ago when it was a tiltyard. Imagine,' said Lawrence, 'Henry VIII and his courtiers disporting themselves on magnificently caparisoned horses, all demonstrating their prowess. One of the very first things the King did when the palace came into his possession was to lay out nine acres of tiltyards. Five towers were erected here for the spectators and additional pavilions were set up, all highly decorated with banners and tapestries. Great processions were led by the Marshal of the Jousts in his golden robes accompanied by thirty footmen who were followed by trumpeters and drummers. Finally Henry, fully armed wearing a surcoat of silver bawdakin, entered the lists. Henry, as a young man,' he said wistfully, 'his horses flying, would have been a fantastic sight, poetry in motion. You know, James, we'll never see that sort of splendour, it's now all in the mind.

'Lawrence, when you come down to earth, I need a comprehensive report of everything that happened before you reached the Queen's Apartments. How many in your party? Who was in front of you? Who followed on behind? Where were the warders?'

The American laughed. 'Brenda's always saying I live in the past. Now, let me think, we all entered the Great Hall together, then I gave a running commentary, possibly fifteen minutes. Very sketchy, you understand.'

Byrd smiled to himself. He knew Professor Lawrence Berkeley was always longwinded, knew too that he always relived the past in the telling.

'There were a couple of people ahead of us. After we'd seen the Great Hall we all trooped through the small Horn Room, and rather than gum up the works for any visitors behind us we all congregated in the Great Watching Chamber. At that point one of the sightseers ahead of us fell, completely blocking the exit from the Chamber. Doc went to help. While we stayed put I gave the party a short explanation about the restoration of the ceiling and the arms and badges of Henry VIII and Jane Seymour. Doc took his time. The young woman, who Dwight later said may have been a Cypriot, had twisted her ankle. The attendant was all for calling one of her colleagues whose specific job was first aid, but both Doc and the young lady said it was unnecessary.'

'How badly hurt was she?'

'Nothing much. A slight sprain, nothing broken.'

'And her companion, was he a Cypriot?'

'Could have been. They were both most grateful to Doc. Too effusive, I thought, but the young lady limped back the way she'd come, so I guess she was feeling pretty uncomfortable.'

'You carried on?'

'Yes. By the time we got moving again there was no one ahead of us.'

'What time was this?'

'About twelvish. It took us, roughly speaking, another half an hour before we reached the Queen's Presence Chamber.'

Byrd stood for some moments gazing, at a rich, bold,

scarlet rose; Invincible, the tag read. Is that an omen, he wondered?

'Did you see any warders in the Queen's Apartments?'

'No, not until Mrs Spratt showed up and she, poor soul, fainted when she realised Doris Veasey was dead.'

'Tell me about your party.'

'Not a lot to tell. They're all members of the New Jersey Tudor Society which means they can trace their ancestry back to Tudor England.'

'Sounds a bit esoteric. How on earth did you get involved?'

'Marilyn de Grey, who was at Princeton, asked me as a favour if I'd spend the week with them. Remunerated, of course. Wish now I'd refused, but never again, that goes for a coach tour too.'

'Are you positive you all entered the Great Hall together?'

'Absolutely certain.'

In Hanwell-on-the-Hill Jane Stormont was also certain. Certain that the extension ladder they kept in the garage had been moved. She'd collected the twins from school in the nearby village of Hornton before driving into Banbury to do her Thursday shop at Sainsburys. The window cleaner? Had he used it? Unlikely. He came once a month and always on Mondays. What about Anna, her nextdoor neighbour? Not on. If Anna had wanted to borrow it she would have said. Perhaps it was foolish to leave the upstairs windows open? She'd close them in future. Better leave the children playing in the garden while she looked round the house. Burglars sometimes did horrific, unspeakable things.

Unlocking the front door she stepped into the hall dreading what she might see. Cautiously she opened Pete's study door on the left of the hall. Thank God, it was as she'd left it. The dragon cars Pete had made for the children were still on the window seat, and the Cathedral board game he'd just sold for a goodly sum to Boddingtons was on the desk where she'd left it. Quickly she went from room to room. Was there anything out of place? No, everything as it was two hours ago. She took a deep breath and slowly climbed the stairs. All the bedroom doors were open, so too was her office, but the bathroom was closed. Surely she'd left every door wide open to get the house aired? Don't imagine things. Just look. Nothing, absolutely nothing out of place in any of the rooms. She opened the bathroom door. Didn't seem to be anything amiss, maybe the junk on the windowsill looked too tidy. Toothpaste, toothbrushes, face cream, talcum powder, a bath cap and a bowl of potpourri all carefully positioned on the left of the sill. The area in front of the open window was clear. Odd that, but no sign of entry. Her imagination, once again, working overtime. Thankfully she went downstairs and called the children in for tea.

Detective Superintendent Byrd, who still hadn't made contact with Inspector Mozart, spoke with all the Americans, except one, who merely repeated what the Professor had said. Doc Jackson, despite being upset about the way his wife had taken herself off, was most helpful. He was almost certain that Doris Veasey had died some time between twelve noon and one o'clock. Fortuitous, thought Byrd, one doesn't usually find a doctor on the spot, and one so eager to help. When he was sure there was nothing more to be gleaned from the Americans he asked the Professor to assemble his troops and get moving. No need to keep them hanging about.

Mrs Spratt looked smart in her navy-blue uniform, red-banded cap and sheer black stockings. Bleached blonde hair protruded from under her cap, and her large brown eyes, slightly bloodshot from crying, looked directly into the compassionate eyes of the man facing her. She was now fully in control and wouldn't cry again until the day of the harrowing funeral.

'Tell me, Mrs Spratt, every single thing you can remember about today, from the moment you came on duty.'

'There was nothing untoward, Superintendent. All the tourists who visited the Great Hall and the Queen's Apartments were total strangers, apart from two men I've seen before. I can't put a name to either, but I'm sure I've seen the older one on the box. Could be a politician, I suppose, but I've definitely seen the younger man. He occasionly strolls in the grounds with Lady Stormont.'

'Lady Stormont! Who's she?'

'Lives in one of the Grace and Favour apartments. Very elegant lady in her mid-sixties.'

'Do you know which flat?'

'Not quite sure, but I think she overlooks the knot garden. I believe the two men were talking business.'

'Why's that?'

'They weren't really looking, weren't interested, they just stood there gassing. Peggy asked them if they wanted to hire cassettes, but the older man declined. They were followed by a tall young woman who did hire one. I'm sure she was the only person anywhere near them as they went round. Shortly after that there was a slight accident. A young woman slipped, but an American doctor coped with that, and as she adamantly refused to let me call for first aid I did no more about it. That's all I can tell you. Sorry I can't be more help . . . but . . . no . . . I don't suppose its of any . . .'

'Go on.'

'Well, it may not be of interest but Doris and I changed places halfway through our stint. She wanted to go to the loo at the far end, so I took over in the Watching Chamber. Just as well because I was actually on the spot when the girl slipped. Couldn't bring an action against us because it was her own fault for wearing those awful espadrilles.'

'An action?'

'Yes. We're covered, of course, by Central Funds, but I can assure you there's not a floorboard or tile out of place anywhere in the palace.'

'Did you manage to hear what the two men were talking about?'

'Not really. I caught one phrase which made me think of a Spielberg film. The younger man muttered something like "so much for EW", and I immediately thought of ET, you know, the Extra-Terrestial.'

'Yes, I know,' said Byrd who'd taken his daughter Kate to see it, not once, but thrice. 'You've been most helpful, Mrs Spratt.'

She looked at him and shook her head. 'What I can't believe, sir, is that Doris, of all people, actually climbed into that bed. She must have had a brainstorm.'

As the coach eased its way into the heavy traffic on the M25 the Professor who had finished reading the second of two recent publications on Monmouth, breathed a sigh of contentment and stretched his long legs. The last lap of an interminable week. Only Marilyn de Grey and the Dudleys from Morristown had kept him sane. Colin and Freda were both solicitors working in a large practice. Freda was in charge of the conveyancing section and Colin specialised in litigation. Their irrepressible sense of fun, and good humour had enlivened dinner each evening. Colin's ancestors were, as he explained, definitely below the salt with no connections whatsoever to Robert Dudley, Earl of Leicester, so beloved by Queen Elizabeth. His antecedents were coal miners and Puritans from Dudley in the Black Country who fled from Staffordshire and boarded the *Mayflower*.

Lawrence glanced round the coach; everyone seemed

happy enough, everyone except Dwight Jackson. The doctor, sitting across the gangway, was slumped in his seat. Only the constant rubbing of his thumbs hard against the tips of his fingers gave any outward sign of his inward disquiet. Throughout the trip his wife, Sarah, had made her protest not by shouting or histrionics, but by sitting mute making it quite clear that a seven-day whistlestop tour around England wasn't her sort of holiday. Now she'd gone the whole hog and made her own way back to the Hilton. Another quiet protest.

Neither the doctor nor his wife had raised their voices in the Professor's hearing. That's why he'd not believed Judy Devereaux when she said they'd had one hell of a slanging match.

James Byrd watched as the coachload of Americans and their erudite guide were driven out through the Trophy Gate before making his way to Abrams' office musing on the scenario he was trying to create from the modicum of information he'd gathered. EW? Was EW a person, a firm, or a product? What sort of business were the two men discussing, and could the young woman who slipped be part of the picture?

He found the Captain sitting at his desk glancing through the afternoon mail. He motioned Byrd to a comfortable seat near the window.

'Difficult to concentrate, Mr Byrd. The phone hasn't stopped, and although Miss Moorcroft has fielded most of the calls, I've still had to deal with the most temerarious correspondents on the nationals. The crowd at the gates has been dispersed, but there's still a couple of persistent reporters in the car park refusing to budge.'

Suddenly Byrd realised what the acronym EW meant.

'Captain, why should two men choose to stroll round the interior of the palace discussing Electronic Warfare?'

'Talking about recent events in the Gulf War?'

'Maybe. Mrs Spratt heard the younger man say "so much for EW" which doesn't give us much of a clue.'

'Clue! Of course. I'm a bit slow off the blocks. I heard he'd arrived.'

'Who?'

'Sir Hubert Morrissey, no less.'

'And his companion?'

'Peter Stormont, an inventor, son of Lady Stormont who resides in one of our Grace and Favour apartments.'

'Does her son live with her?'

'No, not permanently, but I believe he's spent quite a bit of time here recently.'

'Morrissey's the Minister of Defence, isn't he?'

'Yes, he's been here several times. The visits follow a pattern. The two men walk round the garden for an hour before lunch, which I presume is a working lunch, then carry on with their discussions until the Minister leaves, usually about three o'clock.'

'Stormont may have seen something Mrs Spratt missed. I'd like a word with him.'

The shrill peep of the phone disturbed Byrd's train of thought. Abrams picked it up automatically as he made a pencil note in his desk diary. Byrd knew by the slight tightening of the muscles round his jaw that he was far from pleased with the report.

'Thank you, Sergeant, I'll see that Inspector Mozart gets your message. We'll expect to hear from you first thing in the morning.' He slowly replaced the phone.

'That was the Coroner's Officer, Superintendent. Poison, as they suspected. A sample has been sent to Dr Patel at Forensic who will get down to work straight away. Hopefully we'll know the result in the morning. I've been on to the BBC. They're broadcasting a message on the World Service following the late news asking Doris Veasey's parents to contact us. If they ring, what on earth do I tell them? Say she was found dead in bed, and the hospital is carrying out a post mortem. The findings may be known in the morning. It's cool, not totally accurate, but there'll be traumas enough when they return home. Their lives will never be the same again.'

Tom Abrams thought about his mother, remembered the effect of an early-morning call. A policeman arriving, knocking at the door, being invited in, and how he, only three at the time, had peered at his mother and the policeman from upstairs through the bannister rails. The Malayan strife was over, had been for six weeks, when his father, an army captain, drove a jeep through the jungle. A puncture caused it to swerve off the road and detonate a hidden land mine. There was little left of either the jeep or his father. For a few seconds his mother whimpered like an animal in pain, and then sat at the bottom of the stairs, not crying, not speaking. He remembered being too frightened to move. The policeman went next door and returned with Mrs Beveridge who helped his mother into the front room, sat her down on the sofa and made her drink sweetened tea. Only then did he creep downstairs and into her arms.

'Superintendent,' said Abrams briskly, trying to erase the memory, 'I'll take you over to Lady Stormont's apartment right now.'

The Superintendent was intrigued by this man's quiet authority, by his grip on the situation. There'd been no need to defer Stephie's birthday celebrations, this man with help from Twickenham could have dealt with any situation.

'Were you army or navy, Captain?'

'Army. SAS.'

Byrd laughed. 'You must find life here exceedingly dull.'

'Well, there's no flying around the universe and being

dropped into unknown locations and dicey situations. It was good while it lasted, but it's a young man's world.'

'You find there's enough here to interest you?'

'Good God, yes. Every day is different, and the human race causes us all manner of headaches, it keeps us on our toes.'

'And you live here?'

'Yes. Look through the window, cast your eye on that Georgian pile. That's been my home for the past ten years.'

Lady Stormont opened the door. Abrams effected an introduction on the threshold before jogging back to the office.

Peter Stormont was sitting on a superb William IV sofa sipping a Tio Pepe. His mother had all the time in the world, nothing would hurry her. She sat the policeman down, talked about the superb weather, gave him a dry sherry in a crystal glass heavy enough to be used as a paperweight, and eulogised over the views from her window. Peter looked on, highly amused, knowing the policeman wanted to get on with whatever it was he had in mind.

'You've arrived at the right time, Mr Byrd. I'm trying to persuade this son of mine, who's a most competent musician, to bring his village brass band down here for our pageant in a month's time. He thinks young people would rather hear folk or pop, but I'm quite sure the whole world loves a brass band, in the right setting, of course. Don't you agree?'

'I'm biased.'

'What do you mean?'

'I'm not a bandsman, Lady Stormont, but occasionly I play the sax.'

'Excellent,' shouted Peter. 'You're my man.'

Both Lady Stormont and her visitor looked at each other in astonishment.

'A saxophone would make all the difference in the world.'

'What are you talking about, Peter?' His mother was distinctly puzzled.

'Our repertoire is the usual run-of-the-mill music we prepare for festivals and village fêtes, but we could improve on that. If we decided to come down here we'd have a fortnight in which to practise new orchestrations of eighteenth-century music, all introducing the sax which is an instrument not usually associated with brass bands. But to do that we need a saxophonist. How about it, Superintendent?'

The enthusiasm and the ebullience of the man appealed to Byrd.

'Let me say, straight away, I am not a virtuoso. I'm a plodder, and I would need plenty of practice.'

'No difficulty. Where do you live, Superintendent?'

'Bletchingdon near Oxford. I'm with Thames Valley Police.'

'Better and better. I live in Hanwell-on-the-Hill, about eighteen miles north of you.'

'I know it well. The Tudor Castle and The Little Dog Laughed.'

'We have two band practices every week on Thursday evenings and Sunday mornings, both in the village hall. Could you make any of them?'

Lady Stormont looked at him anxiously. If he agreed, she knew the band would play. Byrd felt tempted, but he saw too little of his family. One more commitment, even though it would give him undiluted pleasure, would upset Stephanie. He'd not played the sax for nearly two years, not since he'd worked on the Tower case, but his marriage had to be nursed. He'd tried to keep things together by moving out of Oxford soon after the Tower case. Thought village life might be better for both Kate and Stephie.

'I do have a wife and daughter to think . . .'

'Bring them too.' Lady Stormont was decisive. 'They can come and have lunch here, treat the place like home, and enjoy the festivites.'

'OK,' said the willing saxophonist, 'you're on.'

'Now, Mr Byrd, you didn't come to discuss music, so how can we help you?'

Pamela Stormont sat down and took stock of this unconventional policeman who'd arrived in jeans and a quite noticeable shirt.

'I'm here, Lady Stormont, to investigate the circumstances surrounding Doris Veasey's death.'

'Quite extraordinary, Mr Byrd, in fact you could say bizarre. Unfortunately I never met the lady, so I can't help you.'

'No, Lady Stormont, I'm sure you can't, but your son can.'

'You want to know,' said Peter, 'if I noticed her asleep in the four-poster?'

'How did you hear about this?' asked the Superintendent quickly.

'On the four o'clock newsflash. Didn't say much, merely a short statement reporting that a body had been discovered in a four-poster at Hampton Court Palace. Mother rang Miss Moorcroft who gave her the lowdown. If Mrs Veasey's body was there when Sir Hubert and I walked through the room then I'm afraid we both missed out.'

'Do you remember any of the visitors, any detail at all, however small?'

'Not really, we were concentrating on other matters. Half a minute,' he said closing his eyes. 'Three people followed us into the Great Hall. There was a woman immediately behind us, don't remember her face, but I do recall a mop of black curly hair . . . jeans, she was wearing jeans, and a shapeless shirt . . . and carrying a plastic bag. I am almost certain she hired a cassette. Can't remember a thing about the other two.'

'For someone who can't remember, you've done rather well. How about warders? Were there any around?'

'Yes, I believe there were. I vaguely remember seeing a man and two women, but I can't remember exactly where. You know,' said Peter suddenly, 'I don't believe she was in the bed, something would have clicked. I've been through there so often.'

'Would I be correct in assuming,' asked Byrd, plunging straight into deep waters, 'that your meeting with the Minister of Defence was of national importance?'

'It was.'

'Who else would be interested?'

'Difficult to say.'

'I need a lead, Mr Stormont.'

'It's highly secret. I'm not at liberty to . . .'

'In that case, I only hope that what you said this morning about EW isn't vital.'

'Good God!' Peter looked stunned. 'What are you saying?'

'I believe your conversation was recorded.'

'But the palace isn't bugged.'

'Doesn't have to be.'

'Are you saying that . . .'

'Yes.'

'How could anyone know we'd be in the Queen's Apartments at that particular time?'

'That's what I have to find out, but equally you could have been recorded anywhere . . . in the gardens . . . Fountain Court . . . Clock Court.'

Peter looked at his mother. Without a word she gave a slight nod and made a graceful retreat.

'It's ironic,' said Peter gazing at a large oil painting of his grandfather, 'it's ironic because the entire caboodle, every paper, every equation, and all the drawings were handed to the Minister this afternoon. The project, as far as I'm concerned is over, and I'm on to the next.'

'I suggest you think objectively, try to remember exactly what you said.'

Peter Stormont walked to and fro in the sitting-room while Byrd admired the proportions and elegance of Sir Christopher Wren at his best.

'I think we discussed *Lichtenstein*, and Freya, which have nothing . . .'

'Lichtenstein? Freya?'

'*Lichtenstein*, an airborne radar, built by Telefunken, was used by the Germans during the war. It was launched in 1942, suffered electronic teething problems, but eventually proved a winner until we found a way to jam the beams. *Freya*, named after a Scandinavian goddess is another system which we also managed to counteract once we discovered the enemy was using 570 megacycles. We received the signals, modulated them and sent them back. A brilliant piece of engineering which we called "Moonshine". One aircraft carrying "Moonshine" could simulate the echo of squadrons flying in formation. Think what nine planes could do, and did. It was a great spoof, Superintendent, which was used again and again to divert the enemy's attention from the genuine attack. All this is history, of course, but it is germane to our present project, but useless to an eavesdropper because anyone can pick up this information in an excellent book on radar by Alfred Price. In fact, Superintendent, we must have been virtually inaudible at times because we were whispering. Good God!'

'What's the matter?'

'I distinctly remember standing, for some minutes, near one of the female warders. Are you saying she recorded us?'

'Describe her,' barked Byrd.

'Not very tall, about five three or four.'

'Hair?'

'Short, blonde, not much showing. Her hands, I noticed her hands.'

'Yes?'

'She was wearing two enormous costume rings, one on each hand, as well as a wedding ring.'

'And where at this time was the visitor with the mop of curly hair?'

'Not far behind, always with her back to us, standing by the window in the next room.'

'Which room was that?'

'The Queen's Guard Chamber.'

'Could you see the two people, a young man and woman, who entered the Great Hall at the same time as the lady with the mop of hair?'

'No.'

Both men heard the phone ringing in the hall.

'It's Captain Abrams for you, Superintendent,' said Lady Stormont as she entered.

'Can you get over to the Royal Pew above the Chapel immediately?' asked Abrams. 'It's urgent. I'll meet you there.'

Following Dr Stormont's directions he ran like the wind, down the stairs across the cobbles into Clock Court, through the Great Hall and into the Haunted Gallery. Barricades were already in place at both ends and Abrams was standing at the first entrance to the Royal Pew with two Royal Parks Police Constables and a uniformed Inspector. The elusive Mozart, at last! Not the moment for introductions. He noticed a distraught warder sitting on a bench with his head in his hands.

'It gets worse by the minute,' said Abrams. 'Boyle here,' he said pointing to the warder, 'has found another body.'

'Here!'

'Yep, in one of the ante-chambers. Wilkins, who gave the victim the kiss of life, and Shaw were here within seconds of getting the call but they were too late. Constable

Shaw,' he said indicating the policewoman, 'closed off the area immediately. Nothing has been disturbed except the body.'

'I hadn't any option, sir, in case she was still alive,' blurted Wilkins as he saw the expression on Byrd's face.

'You did what you had to do, Constable, so let's take a look at the corpse.'

He followed the young man, no more than twenty, who'd only been in the Force for six months.

'There she is, sir, still warm. I turned her over to give her the kiss of life, but it wasn't any good, sir. She was . . .' His voice trembled.

'You did very well, Constable. Get Boyle here.'

The man came slowly, didn't want to look at the body. He felt sick, physically sick.

'How long had you been on duty, Mr Boyle?' asked Byrd.

'Nearly two hours, sir.'

'Been a lot of people through?'

'Yes, sir.'

'How many?' barked Abrams who was angry at the man's incompetence.

'A hundred, give or take a few.'

'Mugged, perhaps,' murmured Mozart.

'No, sir. Her handbag's behind the screen. I haven't touched it,' said Wilkins quickly. 'Forensic will need it, won't they, sir?'

'Every little helps,' said the Superintendent, whose mind was working overtime.

'Seen any Mediterranean types around?' he asked, looking at the warder. 'Could be Cypriots.'

'No, sir. Only a party of Japanese, two West Indians, and a guy on his own, Italian, I think.'

'Constable, pick up the handbag and bring it here. Use your handkerchief.'

'Haven't got one.'

'Here take mine,' growled Mozart.

Wilkins lifted the handbag with the tip of his finger, and using the handkerchief managed to extract a brown leather wallet containing money and cheque cards which he handed to the bearded, badly dressed senior officer. Byrd carefully removed an American Express card.

'Sarah Jackson . . . Jackson?'

That rang a bell. Less than an hour had elapsed since he'd heard the lady who indulged in eclairs telling the Professor that Sarah and Dwight Jackson were missing. Sarah Jackson, she'd said, had rowed with her husband and threatened to take a taxi to the Hilton at Heathrow. Byrd unzipped the back of the wallet. The three men stared at a wodge of notes.

'Not short of a bob or two, was she!' said Mozart. 'I reckon there's two hundred quid there.'

'She was an American, on holiday, here to enjoy herself,' said Byrd bitterly. 'Her husband's the doctor who examined Doris Veasey. At the moment he's on his way to the Hilton.'

'You clairvoyant, Superintendent?' said Abrams.

'No, but in the right place, at the right time for once.'

Not as far as I'm concerned, you're not, thought Mozart.

Byrd knelt down and looked closely for bruising on the dead woman's neck.

'Not a mark on her. Strange, she doesn't have the look of a person whose been asphyxiated. What do you make of it, Captain?'

'Could have been a Chinese chop to the neck, not leaving a mark, like we were taught in the Corps. It's quick. No time for the victim to cry out, so why the plastic bag?'

'Dunno, but we need a doctor here pronto to pronounce life extinct then the body can be taken straight to Kingston for a post mortem, or to Hammersmith if they're too busy.'

'No problem,' said Abrams, 'I've already contacted Dr Kelsoe, he's on his way.'

'Inspector Mozart, you'd better make sure the Forensic boys don't leave. Get them over here straight away.'

'Will do,' said the Inspector, as he turned on his heel, unable to bring himself to say 'sir'.

At 15.00 as Inspector Mozart, whom the Force at Twickenham had nicknamed Wolfgang, was about to go off duty he'd been ordered by Chief Superintendent Platt to Hampton Court Palace. He was annoyed, it messed up the arrangements he'd made with his old man. He'd planned to pick him up at four o'clock, and drive over to Imber Court Sports Club where they'd spend a pleasant couple of hours playing bowls. The weekly exercise during the summer had begun as a duty, but now the Inspector, who was nearing fifty, found it a pleasant relaxation, away from the station, away from the phone. Bliss. A corpse in the Royal Pew at the palace was the last thing he needed. They'd called in that brash Superintendent from Thames Valley. Let him get on with the job.

James Byrd, on his way back to the office, checked the distance from the Royal Pew to the Queen's Presence Chamber where the first victim was found. Meantime Inspector Mozart had organised the Forensic boys who hadn't shown any enthusiasm, who both thought they'd done enough for one day.

Miss Moorcroft, who'd finished for the day, told the Inspector, whom she knew well, to make himself at home in her office. He settled down to make meticulous notes and wait for the magician, who had only to wave his magic wand, and the case would be solved.

He took one look at Byrd when he entered, thinking that everything he'd heard about the man was true. The dark hair and the beard made him look more like a swashbuckling corsair than a policeman. The way he dressed, the casual arrogance, told him in a flash that this murder investigation wouldn't be played by the book, neither would it be a fleeting visit by a man who was a thorn in the flesh of Chief Superintendent Keating at Thames. Byrd knew what Mozart was feeling, knew what he would have felt in the circumstances. As he entered the room he held out his hand.

'Glad to meet you, Inspector. Glad there's someone around who knows this place inside out. Just what I need.'

The maverick policeman sat down and picked up the phone to ring Professor Berkeley. There was a long wait. 'Come on,' he muttered, 'get your act together.'

Lawrence was stunned when he heard Sarah Jackson had been murdered.

'Why in heaven's name did it have to happen today? Why didn't he wait till he got back to the States?'

'To do what?'

'Murder his wife.'

'Lawrence, you're jumping the gun.'

'Of course Dwight Jackson did it. They've hardly spoken a word for the past seven days. Aren't the majority of crimes marital?'

'No one is guilty, Lawrence until . . .'

'I know.'

The Professor was even angrier when the entire coach party was asked to remain for a further twenty-four hours, to give Byrd and Mozart a chance to question them.

'There'll be a police car at the hotel in a few minutes to bring you and the doctor back to the palace.'

Lawrence's expletives rent the air. Quite a turn of phrase for a historian, thought the Superintendent.

In the meantime two Forensic officers were hard at work in the Royal Pew. They lifted the small dark-haired woman who had eschewed make-up, and placed her in a body bag before making a sweep of the entire area. They found little of interest apart from her dark glasses which must have come off as the murderer put the bag over her head.

Byrd's second call was to Sir Elwyn's deputy at the Met, who ordered him to remain in charge of both murder enquiries.

Never change horses in midstream, was one of Sir Elwyn's maxims which his deputy knew full well. His third call was more difficult, difficult too in front of Mozart, and Stephanie didn't help.

'It'll take more then twenty-four hours,' he said.

'What did you expect? You should always travel with your toothbrush and pyjamas. Be prepared, isn't that your motto? You should have been a boy scout.'

'I'll let you know . . .'

'There's no need. We'll expect you when we see you . . . nothing changes.'

'I'm sorry, Stephie.'

'Don't be sorry. You'll find life easier in future.'

'Why's that?'

'I've an appointment in the morning with a solicitor.'

'Solicitor!' Byrd's voice was no more than a whisper.

'Yes, to initiate divorce proceedings.'

'Cancel it. Let's talk.'

'We've talked too much.'

'Give it a week before you do anything. A divorce is not the answer. Maybe changing my job is . . . teaching languages . . .'

'You've said that before.'

'We'll talk as soon as I get back.'

'This year, next year, sometime never . . .' She put the phone down.

Inspector Mozart made no move. He sat listening, smiling to himself. Not being married he didn't have all these problems which half the Force had to face. A worried Byrd, with a wife screaming for divorce, might just botch up the case. Yes, that would be a most satifying outcome, make him a very happy man.

3

Lawrence Berkeley stood outside Room 204 waiting for Dwight Jackson to answer his peremptory knock.

'Where've you been?' shouted the doctor as he opened the door. His face fell as he looked up at the man who towered above him. 'Sorry, Professor, sorry. I thought you were Sarah.'

A good actor, this one, thought Lawrence as he walked straight into the room without waiting to be asked. He noticed the bottle of whisky and half-filled glass on the bedside table. He saw too that the doctor had been lying on the bed. Lying on the bed waiting for what? News of his wife's death?

Dwight Jackson closed the door recognising in the body language and tenseness of his visitor that this was no social call.

'What's up, Professor?'

Lawrence looked at him slightly puzzled, not knowing where to start.

'It's Sarah, isn't it? She's flown back home. Never thought she'd do it . . . threatened several times . . . but she's not taken anything with her . . . that's why I didn't think she'd gone.'

The Doctor's shrill tones echoed round the room.

'Sit down, Dr Jackson, sit down.'

Suddenly the doctor was uneasy. What had Sarah done? She always lived on her nerves . . . quite unpredictable at times . . . but he usually managed to calm her down. It was this damn coach trip. They should never have come.

'We have to return to Hampton Court . . . there's a police car waiting.'

'Why? What has she done?'

'I'm sorry, doctor, to have to tell you this . . .' Lawrence hesitated, he almost believed that the grey-haired balding man sitting in front of him was unaware, but he couldn't be. Why had he been on edge, and why had he fidgeted nervously throughout the entire journey back to the Hilton? Something must have been bugging him.

'Doctor, I'm sorry to be the bearer of appalling news . . . there is no other way of telling you this . . . there are no words . . . your wife, I'm afraid, is dead.'

'Sarah dead?' he whispered, and shook his head again and again.

Lawrence nodded at the man, who in a space of a few seconds appeared to be smaller and older and totally unrecognisable as the competent doctor, who only three hours before had pronounced Mrs Veasey dead.

'How? How did she do it?'

The Professor could no longer look into the tortured eyes of the stricken man. He moved slowly towards the window.

'Superintendent Byrd didn't say.'

'But she's not the type, Professor. Nearly everyone threatens at some time or other, but with Sarah it was only for effect . . . she never meant to take her life . . . she never meant it . . .'

The journey from the Hilton to the palace took longer than expected. A lorry had jack-knifed, totally blocking the eastbound traffic. It was some time before the police driver could extricate himself from the snarl-up which ensued. Dwight Jackson sat with his eyes closed, not uttering a word throughout the entire journey. Nothing mattered any more . . . the swimming pool was nearly finished . . . the pool Sarah had set her heart on . . . she planned to swim every day . . . keep fit . . . he'd never use it now . . . and the house she'd persuaded him to buy . . . far too big for them . . . what good was it all?

Lawrence fought hard to think of other matters, trying not to dwell on the unhappiness of the man beside him.

He concentrated his mind on Cambridge, on a carefully planned vital exchange of roles which had given a new impetus to his life. So too had his marriage at the age of fifty to Brenda. Colleagues at Princeton warned him it wouldn't last. Wasn't he a confirmed bachelor, a recluse who spent his leisure time in a remote spot in the Adirondack Mountains? A retreat where he could enjoy his favourite pastime of fishing, a place where he could read and write without interruption. No telephone. No television. Only a radio. But everything had changed since his visit to the Tower of London, two years ago, where he'd spent a month with Brenda and Steve at 5 Tower Green, albeit under false pretences. After Steve's body had been found in a tunnel under the house he'd come clean. Superintendent Byrd had seen to that, but Brenda, always a lonely woman, had implored him to stay on, keep her company in an ancient house full of ghosts. That was the beginning of a relationship based on a desperate need for companionship. He'd never realised or faced his own solitary state until he understood how Brenda suffered. No great protestations of love, they were both afraid of that. It was only as the traffic began to move again that he realised a seed had been sown and was blossoming.

Brenda must never know why he'd engineered the Cambridge exchange. *There are more things in heaven and earth, Horatio*. She must go on thinking the three-year stint in England is giving her a chance to see something of her sister.

Professor Kettle had been quite surprised to see him, had been quite taken aback when they shook hands like old friends. Was even more surprised when the American had congratulated him on his excellent monograph. Kettle rather self-consciously laughed it off.

'Ideas, my dear fellow, often travel on the ether, erupt at the same time.'

An affirmation of guilt, thought Lawrence, from the man who when he'd met him at that damned symposium four years ago had never had anything published, not even a pamphlet. A man who shamelessly plagiarised his notes on Francis Bacon which he was fool enough to let him read. Kettle's monograph appeared in Britain six weeks before Princeton published his own work which had taken him ten long years to research. A work in which he proved to his own satisfaction that Bacon was the son of a morganatic marriage between Elizabeth and Leicester. After Kettle's success, which was eulogised in academic circles on both sides of the Atlantic, his own meticulous study was an anti-climax.

Sold down the river.

Kettle, as though wanting to atone for his crime, courted him, invited him to social events, always quizzing him about his present research, and reiterating again and again how ideas like dandelion seeds are borne on the wind. Lawrence smiled to himself. He'd not divulged too much, merely enough to whet Kettle's appetite. However, as Kettle had remarked when they sat next to each other at High Table at Clare, 'All's fair in love and war.'

The dinner was excellent and the wine superb. Lawrence mentioned, quite casually, during the fish course that he was working on an original idea, a seventeenth-century subject, a subject which would rock the establishment, offend the royalists.

'Nothing,' said Kettle, 'absolutely nothing could rock the British Institution, especially an event in the seventeenth century.'

'Don't you be too sure,' grinned Lawrence.

After dinner he'd forgotten to pick up his briefcase from

under his chair in the hall. Carelessness attributable, perhaps, to an excess of excellent claret. Kettle had ushered him towards the Senior Combination Room where coffee was being served, introduced him to a colleague, and then excused himself saying he had an urgent phone call to make. He was gone at least twenty minutes. Only as the Professor was leaving did he remember to collect his briefcase. Remembered too that Kettle had been absent . . . plenty of time to photocopy the lot, but would he have the nerve to do a repeat performance?

Two weeks after the meeting at High Table Professor Berkeley had dined at the Garrick Club. It was everything he'd expected. A totally English establishment . . . nowhere like it in the world. Every wall covered with portraits of great actors, the greatest being Garrick; there were pictures of scenes from plays, and an abundance of playbills. He made his way past the central table, where twenty members were already seated, in a dining-room smaller than he'd imagined, to the corner where publishers gather. Another tradition peculiar to the Garrick. There he spent a fruitful couple of hours with the director of University Books discussing the jacket cover, price, and date for the publication of his book on Monmouth. It was a machiavellian decision on both sides to leave the date open.

Lawrence decided to return to Hampton Court Palace as soon as the Tudor Society was out of his hair, see what else he could dig up about Monmouth. After all, the eldest of Charles II's thirteen royal bastards must have spent a considerable amount of time at the palace where his father, in the early years of his reign, had restored the tennis courts, and Monmouth being a great sportsman would have played tennis, hunted and womanised at the palace, which for him was the greatest game of all.

At the very moment the police driver drove the car

through the Lion Gates, on the hottest June day for fifty years, the news reached the Yorkshire Dales. The Administrator and his wife found the heat overpowering, enervating, and had cut short their fifteen-mile circuitous walk, and returned to base shortly before six o'clock. While Lady Wishart, who was slightly hard of hearing, sat glued to the box listening to the six o'clock news her husband was sitting in the bath massaging his tired feet. He was concentrating on reducing the inflammation affecting his big toe when he heard the newscaster mention Hampton Court Palace. In a trice he was out of the bath and into the bedroom.

'You're dripping water everywhere.'

'Shush. I want to hear.'

Early this afternoon a body was discovered in a four-poster bed in the Queen's Presence Chamber at Hampton Court Palace by a party of American tourists.

'My God, why hasn't Tom called me?'

'Because,' said his wife, 'you told him we'd be out until seven each evening.' He dashed back into the bathroom, grabbed a towel, dried himself and got dressed.

'We'll have to get back as soon as possible.'

'I don't know why you're in such a hurry, people die of heart attacks every day of the week. Tom can cope, you know he can.'

The police driver, who'd had a pig of a journey from the Hilton, stopped briefly at the barrier in Tennis Court Lane. As the car stopped Dwight Jackson opened his eyes and saw two ambulance men unloading a stretcher.

'I've got to see her,' he screamed. 'Where is she?'

The Professor restrained him. 'I've no idea, doctor. We'd better see Superintendent Byrd first. He'll explain.'

'What do you mean . . . explain?'

'I want to know how Sarah . . . I also want to know

why . . .' He shouted at the driver. 'Stop man, and let me get out.'

'We are stopping, sir.'

Inspector Mozart, who'd been warned by the constable on the outer gates, was already in the forecourt. He opened the car door, put his arm round the distraught man, who looked as if he'd collapse at any minute, and ignoring his protestations helped him upstairs into the outer office. Abrams took in the situation at a glance and produced a bottle of brandy from a small cabinet near the window, and poured him a massive tot.

'Drink it,' he commanded.

Dwight Jackson was incapable of holding the glass, his hands and body shook. Mozart held it to his lips as though he were a child, but he pushed it away.

'Come on, doctor,' said the Inspector, 'a sip will do you good. Captain Abrams,' he whispered, 'you'd better get Kelsoe over here straight away.'

He nodded and slipped quietly into Colonel Wishart's office to use his walkie-talkie.

The Professor couldn't stomach all this, he ran back down the stairs into the forecourt to get some air. Brenda had shown much more control when Steve was murdered. Perhaps women had more inner strength?

The Superintendent had been busy, so too had Detective Sergeant Georgina Mayhew. Quicker, thought Byrd, to rely on his own staff than expect men he didn't know at the Met to stop what they were doing and carry out his orders. The Sergeant was a competent woman, and dedicated. Since her divorce, there'd been nothing to distract her from a job she really enjoyed doing, but with her looks and figure it won't be long, thought Byrd, before she's ensnared once again. With luck, and her flare for dealing quietly with the most complex cases she should, within the year, make Inspector. Mayhew, he knew, would make sure that all ferries and airports were alerted to keep a look out for three Cypriots, One man and two women who might be travelling together. If they'd no hand in Doris Veasey's murder then they must be eliminated.

'I've got to see her,' shouted Dr Jackson at the bearded policeman sitting behind the Colonel's desk. 'I want to know how she's . . .'

'Sit down, sir.' Inspector Mozart pushed a chair behind the distraught man's knees and with a gentle push on his shoulders sat him down.

'I want to know why.'

'So do I, doctor. I've a few questions, before we both go over to the Chapel,' said Byrd quietly. 'I'll be as brief as I can.'

'A damn stupid way you do things in England. Questions . . . questions. they're not important. Sarah is. How did she do it?'

'Do what, doctor?'

'Kill . . . kill herself.'

'She didn't.'

'What! You mean she's had an accident?'

'No. I'm afraid she was murdered.'

Dwight Jackson stared at the policeman hardly able to comprehend.

'Mugged, mugged, I suppose. It happens all the time in the States, but this is England.'

Byrd took a deep breath. 'She was not mugged, sir. She was found dead with a plastic bag over her head.'

'You mean she suffocated herself!'

'No, doctor. She didn't commit suicide, that's why I have to ask you a few questions.'

Only then did the doctor realise how tense the two policemen were.

'You think I killed her, don't you?'

'I've no idea, sir, who did it, but I need to know where you were between two and four this afternoon?'

The shaken man said nothing. He looked first at Inspector Mozart, standing beside him, as though help might come from that quarter, and then at his inquisitor.

'I'm sorry, sir, to inflict any more pain, but what were you doing?'

'Looking for Sarah.'

'Why? Was she lost?'

She was fed up with this trip . . . hated travelling in the coach . . . swore she'd take a taxi back to the hotel . . . I couldn't believe she meant it . . . that she'd actually gone . . . she so often says these things . . . says the first thing that comes into her head . . . been like this since the menopause started . . . so I thought maybe she was . . . she was . . .'

'Yes?'

'I thought she was making me suffer . . . hiding for a joke, you see, in the maze. But . . .' The grieving man covered his face with his hands, finding it impossible to continue.

Mozart spoke softly. 'Kelsoe's on his way, Superintendent. I don't think Dr Jackson should see the Chapel yet, not in his . . .'

'Chapel!' shouted the American. 'Is Sarah there?'

Byrd nodded. 'In the Royal Pew.'

The American was on his feet. 'Let's get moving, then.'

'You must be prepared, doctor . . .'

'I know what the dead look like . . . I know . . .'

'All right, sir, we'll go now.'

'I'll re-route Dr Kelsoe,' said Abrams.

Byrd gave him a nod. 'Thanks, Captain.'

Peter Stormont drove back to Hanwell-on-the-Hill on a high. His involvement with the MoD over, he could now return to his experiment in Oxford which he'd been pursuing for nearly two years. Special Branch had called off the minders and life would once again revert to normal with Jane and the kids, no longer at risk. Now he could unveil the surprise for the children which he'd kept hidden in the garage. It would only work efficiently on a hot sunny day, with temperatures in the seventies. There was no time like the present. The sun would heat it up before supper, and afterwards with luck they'd see and hear the musical box working. It had taken a lot of patience to reproduce De Caus's sixteenth-century musical toy operated by solar power.

As he neared Banbury, he automatically stopped in a lay-by, took a small bottle from his pocket, loosened the screw top and extracted two Tolbutamide tablets, blessing, as he always did, the fact that he was suffering from a mild form of diabetes which was manageable without recourse to perpetual insulin injections. He sat for some minutes thinking about the weeks ahead. Work that he must complete within the next six months, work that might deplete the wealth of the Middle East, and to some extent Britain, but would, in the long run, benefit mankind. Such a simple idea; three more tests, and he'd be there.

He switched on the ignition and ten minutes later arrived on the outskirts of the village. Plenty of time to set up the toy and run through the scores for the 7.30 band practice. A bit of luck bumping into that policeman. A saxophone would make all the difference in the world. Pity they'd not been allowed to use one in the recent Milton Keynes Brass Band Contest.

His heart sank as he turned through the gates of the Old Rectory and recognised the dark blue BMW parked in the drive. Not today, Paul my friend, this was meant to be family only. Paul Burgess, a man of many interests, and very little time, had somehow managed to put everything aside to do his duty. Recently he'd taken the role of godfather a little too seriously, had been calling at least once a month. Since giving up the Chair at Cambridge where once he'd tutored Peter he was now jet-hopping around the world in his capacity as Chairman of Olio, a powerful international oil company. Damn it, the toy will have to wait.

Peter opened the front door expecting to hear the twins who were always home by 3.30. He stood for a moment listening, the house was never this quiet, then he heard sounds from the kitchen as Jane began emptying the dishwasher.

'Where are they all?'

Jane laughed. 'You may well ask. They're playing hide and seek with Paul, but he's cheated.'

'You mean he only counted to eighty.'

'No. He's not even tried to find them yet. He's secreted himself in the study.'

'What!'

'It's hide and seek in reverse. They're now creeping round upstairs trying to find him.'

There were a few house rules the children had to observe. No TV before four o'clock; bed by eight; no playing in the road, and the study totally out of bounds.

'Jane, how long's this game lasted?'

'Don't know, ten minutes, fifteen minutes.'

'That's long enough. Break it up.'

Peter strode into the study half expecting to find Paul hiding behind the floor to ceiling curtains, or playing with the dragon cars he'd made for the children, but he was sitting at the desk thumbing through the *Middle East Economic Digest*.

'You're cheating, Paul.'

'Yes, yes, of course, but it's giving Jane and me a breather.'

'Does she need one?'

'Don't we all.' Paul smiled disarmingly, 'I'll play your latest game with them. I like to keep abreast of what you're doing. What's it called?' He opened the box on the desk. 'Cathedrals! That's an odd title. You've sold it to Boddingtons, I suppose?'

'Yes. Patent pending.'

'You're home early. Thought you were working on the MoD job?'

'No, everything's been handed over, now it's back to base.'

'Doing what? Still playing around with fuel injection?'

'No. There's no future in that.'

'Then you've decided to concentrate on solar power?'

'Yes.'

They heard Jane calling the children, followed by a stampede as Sandra and Stephen rushed downstairs, and stood in the hall outside the study door.

'You're not allowed in there, Uncle Paul, it's out of bounds,' shouted Stephen.

'Is it? Then I'm sorry. Why don't you introduce me to the Cathedral game before I leave?'

In the Haunted Gallery outside the entrance to the Royal Pew, Boyle stood chatting to Constable Wilkins who'd come at the double when he reported finding the body. He felt sick, had to keep talking, try to get the dead woman out of his mind. He'd reported the matter direct to Captain Abrams, hadn't gone through the usual channels, there was no time for that. He knew, although the Captain never raised his voice, that he was livid. Boyle knew he could say goodbye to the job; a pity because he enjoyed it. He was a gregarious fellow who liked having informative chats with folks from all over the world. Must have been chatting, he thought miserably, when it happened. The CID officer in charge was on his way over. He fought back the bitter tasting bile . . . the same feeling he used to experience when the headmaster sent for him. He froze as he saw Inspector Mozart approaching with two strangers.

Constable Wilkins came to attention and saluted Inspector Mozart. At least Wolfgang looked like a policeman, but he couldn't say the same for the guy with him, the wideboy who'd arrived from Oxford, the Super with the knowhow. But who was the haggard-looking man with them? Boyle knew exactly where and when he'd seen the man before. He whispered as much to PC Wilkins. Byrd took the doctor's arm, and following Mozart steered him gently towards the small ante-chamber to the right of the Royal Pew. The two doors, closed by the murderer which had effectively kept the general public at bay, were now wide open. Byrd, intent on Dwight Jackson's reactions, failed to notice PC Wilkins having a quiet word with the Inspector.

Constable Vera Shaw, who'd always fancied she'd make a good detective, had been sitting in the Royal Pew theorising on how the murderer had managed to close both doors to the cubicle, a part of the ante-chamber which she imagined had been used by royalty as a private confessional. How then had the assassin had enough time to asphyxiate the woman who must have made quite a shindig in a building always chock full of visitors? She was still holding the Sainsbury's plastic bag containing a wig which she'd found in the ladies' toilets at the bottom of the Queen's Staircase. The wig had given her cause for thought, ideas from which to build a fantastic scenario, but the answer was all too simple. It must have been left by one of the actresses rehearsing in the Chapel the previous evening for the midsummer pageant due to take place in less than three weeks. As soon as she heard the outer door open she hurriedly returned to her watching brief beside the body.

Dwight Jackson gave a moan and sank down on his knees beside his dead wife. Tears coursed down his cheeks soaking his shirt. Hardly aware of what he was doing he kept stroking his wife's face. 'Why,' he kept murmuring to himself, 'why?'

Mozart's receiver bleeped. Through all the interference and crackling he could just hear Captain Abrams saying that two men from Forensic and Dr Kelsoe were on their way over.

When Webb and Jones appeared Mozart took them to one side, and with a stage whisper that would have reached the gods, and not missed by Byrd whose hearing was ultra sensitive, explained all about the hippy policeman in casual dress. He was disappointed when he discovered they already knew, like everyone else at Twickenham.

Dr Kelsoe took one look at the kneeling man and with Byrd's help got him on his feet. 'It's all right, sir, I'll take care of him.'

'In that case, doctor, perhaps you could liaise with Inspector Mozart; he'll keep me informed?'

'Yes, yes, of course, Mr . . .'

'Byrd, Superintendent Byrd.'

They come disguised in all shapes and sizes, thought the doctor.

WPC Shaw hovered. It was now or never.

'Excuse me, sir, it's probably nothing, but I found this plastic bag in the Ladies'.'

'Is it important, Constable?'

'Probably not, sir, but it contains a wig, could have been left by an actress after last night's rehearsal.'

Suddenly Shaw felt stupid. Why had she mentioned the bag at all? Why hadn't she just handed it over to Lost Property?

Inspector Mozart guffawed. 'This officer fancies herself as Miss Marples, but she needs to be a bit longer in the tooth. Pie in the sky, Shaw.'

'Is it?' murmured Byrd as the cogs in his brain revolved

at an incredible speed. 'Long and black and curly, is it?'

'Someone playing Charles II,' smirked Wolfgang.

'Yes, sir,' said Shaw, amazed. 'It is long, and black, and curly.'

'Here, let me have a look.'

She took it out of the bag and held it up.

'That's it, Constable. My tall young woman is a man.'

'I'm not clairvoyant, sir,' said Mozart with acid in his voice, 'perhaps you could explain?'

'All in good time. Let's get back to the office, Inspector, and congratulations, Shaw. Give it to Mr Webb here, at least he'll have one prize exhibit.'

'Yes, sir,' said the ambitious constable who omitted to say she'd tried it on.

Mozart was furious. He'd heard from a friend of his at Kidlington about this jumped-up Super who kept everything close to his chest and was constantly being slated for his unorthodox approach. The word had got about that he'd never make Chief Super, his face didn't fit. However, he knew a thing or two, might even surprise his temporary boss!

Tom Abrams had been busy. When the two policemen returned to the Administration Block he led them along a corridor to spacious quarters he'd set up as an Incident Room. Telephones, computer, fax. Everything they needed.

'It's too good for us, Captain Abrams,' said the Superintendent as he examined the Victorian furniture. 'Even a carpet! It doesn't begin to look like an office. There's a feeling of repose here, warmth, not a place where one expects to deal with the problem of a lady who died in an ancient bed, possibly poisoned, and another who was murdered.'

'It was a happy place, Superintendent. It's where Scott

of the Antarctic's widow lived for many years. She loved it here.'

'Good God!' said Mozart. 'He was my hero when I was a lad. I read everything I could about him; I even visited The *Discovery* on the embankment, and the sculpture of him done by his wife.' He stopped suddenly, 'Sorry, I . . .'

'Go on, go on,' said Byrd seeing Mozart in an entirely new light. 'Where's the sculpture?'

'Waterloo Place . . . Lady Scott did a wonderful job . . . never thought I'd actually be in her home.'

Abrams laughed. 'This is only the beginning. Hundreds of famous characters have been residents in the palace. Even Shackleton's widow lived . . .'

'Shackleton,' breathed Mozart. 'Shackleton was a junior officer on The *Discovery*.' He sat down totally bemused.

Lawrence Berkeley heard their voices as he walked along the corridor. He was feeling distinctly edgy. His party should have been off his hands. Another twenty-four hours acting as nursemaid was anathema.

'What's happening to Dwight?' he asked as he entered the room.

Mozart answered, his reverie broken. 'Dr Kelsoe's looking after him, he's under sedation. You've nothing to worry about. Kelsoe's taking him home for the night.'

'What do you mean I've nothing to worry about! I've twenty irate tourists doing their nuts who want to know what's happening.'

'Inspector Mozart with two CID officers will spend tomorrow morning at The Hilton getting statements from them, then they'll be free to leave.'

'That's what I'd like. Freedom to leave right now,' he said belligerently.

'Why not stay a while, Lawrence, listen to a few ideas, put your oar in; an academic mind has its uses.'

Mozart sat up, couldn't believe what he was hearing. An outsider, an American at that, being asked for advice on police matters while he became a looker-on, a damned supernumerary, who would have been better employed playing bowls.

The telephone disturbed his irrational thoughts.

Abrams automatically picked it up, listened for a moment and handed it over to Byrd. 'It's the hospital.'

'Yes. I'm the officer in charge. You've completed the autopsy. That was quick. What's the verdict? I see. Well, give me a rough idea. What! You're quite sure? How? Good God! Yes, I'd like the full report. We'll send an officer down to pick it up. Thanks, and absolutely nothing to the Press.'

He replaced the telephone and looked at the three men.

'You're not going to believe this. Mrs Veasey was murdered, poisoned, as they suspected, but the toxin used sounds like a method from the wildest imaginings of Conan Doyle. Snake venom!'

The three men looked at him in total disbelief.

'The effects are immediate. There's no antidote.'

'But why,' said Abrams, 'why?'

Mozart shook himself, pulled himself together. He'd occasionally passed the time of the day with the lady when he'd been called to the palace to deal with more mundane offences. Always good for a laugh, she was. For you, Doris Veasey, I'll give my all, not let my aggro get between him and me.

'Now, sir, we definitely have two murders on our hands.'

'Damnation,' said Abrams, 'a royal palace where two murders have occurred. It won't help our image.'

'Quite the reverse,' said the Professor. 'They'll be here in their droves, hoping for a third. Better than fiction any day.'

'Now if you'll excuse me, I'll grab a meal and be back within the hour,' said Abrams sharply. 'If you need me, Superintendent, I'm on extension thirty-two.'

'Thank you, Captain.'

'A little informality wouldn't come amiss.' He smiled. 'After all, we're in a similar business, and incidentally, you'll find the guest flat at the end of the corridor ready for you. Room 44B. Suggest you eat in the pub at the south end of the bridge. Quite good nosh.'

'Thanks, Tom, you think of everything.'

There was no sound as Abrams left the room and walked down the stairs. A bonus, thought Byrd to have an ex-member of the SAS on my side.

The Professor, pleased to be involved with events, viewed a few more hours away from the Tudor Society with equanimity. Their incessant questions and desire for fulsome explanations were getting him down.

'Let's get this over with, James, because I'm starving, but I must hear what you have to say, your thought processes always amaze me.'

Wolfgang laughed out loud. He might even take to this American.

'OK. You, Mrs Spratt and Peter Stormont are our three most reliable witnesses, but tomorrow I'm sure Inspector Mozart will turn up others. You, Lawrence, being so tall, had the advantage of being able to see over the heads of your group. We'll want to know . . .'

We'll, thought Wolfgang, that's a change.

'. . . exactly what you noticed ahead of and behind your party. But first of all let's think about Peter Stormont's memories, which his subconscious dredged up. He saw a tall young woman with long black hair . . .'

'That,' interrupted the Inspector who was suddenly inspired, 'was the man in drag who left his wig in the Ladies'? But why didn't he use the Gents'?'

'Because he could leave the wig on if there were any women in there, but in the Gents' he would have been thrown out.'

'Not these days, Mr Byrd, not even at Hampton Court Palace.'

Byrd grinned. Mozart was beginning to mellow.

'Peter Stormont then remembered a blonde female attendant who was wearing several rings. Now both Mrs Veasey and Mrs Spratt are blondes about the same height, but it was Mrs Spratt Stormont had seen because Mrs Veasey wasn't wearing any jewellery, not even a wedding ring.'

'That's because she'd been divorced,' interrupted Wolfgang.

'It was Spratt who gave us a lucid description of the man in drag who was bugging Stormont.'

'But how on earth did he know where Stormont would be?' asked Lawrence.

'We don't know, but we do know that the Minister and Stormont have never before talked within the palace precincts. How did they know, is the crunch question. Once we can find out where the information came from, then I believe we would be some way to solving the case.'

'Do you think the two murders are related?' asked the Professor.

'I've an open mind. I'd rather wait until the autopsy on Sarah Jackson has been carried out.'

'If the doctor did it,' said Wolfgang, 'he had the wit to realise that two murders in the same building on the same afternoon would be accepted as the work of one assassin. Let someone else take the rap.'

The Professor shook his head. 'He's not putting on an act. The trauma he's going through is for real.'

'Don't be too sure,' said Mozart, about to play his ace. 'He was seen sitting on the bench in the Haunted Gallery outside the Chapel earlier this afternoon.'

'What!' roared Byrd. 'Why wasn't I told?'

'Because, sir, this is the first time we've sat down to discuss the case.'

'Don't ever do that again. Dammit, I need to question him again, he'll be useless now after sedation.'

The Professor was amused at the aggro between the two policemen. Not a bad thing; a little friction often produced results.

'Tell me, James, what were the Minister and Stormont discussing?'

'Electronic warfare.'

'My God, so it's espionage!'

'Fortunately no damage was done. They discussed methods used during the Second World War.'

'Ironic!' said Mozart. 'They learnt damn all, and that poor woman died for nothing. Murdered because she could identify the killer, so why didn't Mrs Spratt suffer the . . .'

He didn't finish.

'Oh, my God,' said Byrd, 'how blind I've been.'

Both men looked at him wondering what they'd missed.

'At some stage Mrs Veasey took over from Mrs Spratt while she went to the loo. She was away for only a few minutes because the lavatories for warders are close at hand. Our murderer was aware of a warder there, but his back was to her, and intent on the conversation he never noticed that she'd been replaced for a few minutes by Mrs Veasey. He killed the wrong woman. We'll need to mount a surveillance operation, round the clock, on Mrs Spratt, but it still beats me how, with all those people milling around, the murderer managed to . . .'

'Crystal clear,' said the Professor. 'It happened during the delaying tactics when a young woman sprained her ankle.'

Good on you, thought Mozart. The bearded wonder has been upstaged.

4

A frenzied week of activity following the murders had produced nothing but aggro. Colonel Wishart was back in harness, wisely keeping a low profile, stone-walling the media with great aplomb and tact. He settled down to everyday problems leaving his Head of Security, a way-out ex-member of the SAS, to deal with the aftermath of two murders.

The Press had made a meal of the double murder, both women killed in an ancient building full of visitors who saw and heard nothing, and both the victims of a particularly lethal snake venom. In many murder cases the police can glean information by making door to door enquiries, but tourists who had visited the palace on Black Thursday had vanished into the mist, by jet, by car, by bus, by river boat and on foot. Aggrieved members of the New Jersey Tudor Society were kept hanging around for two days not twenty-four hours as originally envisaged, while Mozart and his minions painstakingly questioned them. *They should have expected it*. The Professor's words. Any man remotely involved with the Tudors had to protect his back and the ladies their heads. Professor Berkeley spent an abortive two days listening to their moans and groans. Mrs Spratt complained she was being followed, felt she was being watched. The attendants were also getting uptight at having their schedules mucked about to enable that bearded policeman, who looked like a corsair, to walk them through everything they'd done on a day they wanted to forget. He even wanted to know exactly where they'd gone at their end of their two-and-a-half-hour shifts. Did they have tea? Who did they see? Who did they remember? Stupid questions. Hundreds of people went through in a day. It was easier to remember groups like the two parties of French children who'd passed through on Thursday morning at the speed of sound hoping to absorb three centuries of architectural splendour in two hours. It was hard on them. The coach delivered them. The coach collected them.

The Foreign Office intervened after complaints from the American Embassy, demanding to know why Dr Jackson was being held? The Home Office made it clear that he was not under duress but being cared for by an English doctor until after the inquest. Then the Home Office Minister became personally involved. Instructions were issued. The inquest must be brought forward, but Sir Elwyn Rees-Davies, who'd unwillingly returned from his short sojourn in Paris, argued that the police case was not ready. The Minister at the Home Office overrode his objections, and gave orders for the inquest on both victims to take place at St James's Palace immediately. As Byrd explained to Stephanie the Coroner at Kingston has no jurisdiction over deaths that occur at Hampton Court or any of the Royal Palaces which come under the domain of Her Majesty. On Day 5 the Coroner for the Crown in session at St James's Palace issued a bland statement covering both murders. *Doris Veasey and Sarah Jackson were both murdered by a person or persons unknown.* The Veaseys were angry. They expected justice. Why should bureaucracy conspire to sweep the murder of their daughter under the carpet? Normally a quiet peaceloving couple they descended on Detective Superintendent Byrd, and left him in no doubt that if the criminal or criminals weren't found they would do everything in their power to mount a campaign.

Byrd too was angry, angry that the inquest had been such a short sharp affair, but thankful that the nationals seemed to be letting them off the hook. The first day it hit the front page, on the second it was on the back, and on the third problems in Russia took over.

Byrd knew, instinctively, that once he'd discovered who'd divulged Sir Hubert Morrissey's movements he'd be playing a different ball game. He accepted the troughs philosophically waiting for the one small clue . . . move the case along . . . get into top gear again. The unhappiest moment came when Dwight Jackson had recovered sufficiently to be questioned in depth. Mozart was right. The doctor had been in the vicinity of the Royal Pew at the time of his wife's murder. He'd been looking for her, thought he caught a glimpse in the Haunted Gallery, thought she'd gone into the Royal Pew, followed her in, couldn't see her, so withdrew and sat on a bench in the Gallery where he could clearly see the exit. If only, wished Byrd, Jackson had persisted. If only . . .

The doctor returned to New Jersey with his wife's body, wondering why he'd ever persuaded Sarah to do the tour. She hated flying. She hated coach trips, and she hated people *en masse*. If only . . .

On the afternoon of day seven Inspector Mozart took a tour of the Queen's Apartments talking to the warders who were on duty at the same time the previous week when the murders were perpetrated. There were only two changes. Mrs Veasey's place had been taken by a temporary warder taken on for the summer season, and Mrs Spratt, who was on sick leave, had been replaced by Boyle. He returned to the office at five o'clock to find that Byrd had already left.

'Early, isn't he?'

'He's gone home, sir,' said Shaw, 'and later if you need him, he'll be in Hanwell-on-the-Hill at band practice.'

'Need him! I need him like a hole in the head.'

* * *

The sixty-mile journey to Bletchingdon gave the Superintendent time in which to mull over events. He'd never felt so impotent over a case, never had so little concrete evidence to show for a week's work. A plastic bag containing a wig. Where did that get him? Instinctively he knew that Peter Stormont was the catalyst, everything stemmed from his conversation with the Minister of Defence. But what happened now? The plans for Tank Evasive Tactics were safely stowed away in the War Office, and Special Branch, who'd been extremely cagey about the affair, had called off their men, didn't want to know, weren't interested. Their decision was hasty, of that he was sure. However, he'd taken steps. Sergeant Mayhew was staying at The Little Dog Laughed in Hanwell. Mozart had been openly derisive about the scheme. A waste of tax payers' money. Mayhew, he knew, had already met Jane Stormont and made some progress, and from a local farmer she'd discovered that the man masquerading as a window cleaner may have been the driver of a white Cavalier. He'd see Mayhew after the band practice, in the pub where she had her ear to the ground.

Problems came thick and fast, his most immediate one was personal. How could he hold his marriage together? His plans for the evening might work, although his motives, as always, were mixed.

He'd no intention of losing the one thing in the world that really mattered. Stephanie, he knew, had been to a solicitor, knew too that she'd do nothing that would affect Kate. The child always came first. Stephie remonstrated with him, said he hardly ever saw his daughter, didn't do his share, shirked his responsibilities. True he'd not seen much of Kate before she started at the village school, always leaving the house before she got up and arriving home after she was in bed. But it was different now. Holidays were bliss, and on his next day off he'd get as far away from the phone as possible. A punt on the *Isis* would do. Perhaps they should have stayed in Oxford? At least Stephie had got out and about as a tour guide during the summer months. There was nothing for her in Bletchingdon, if there were she might be more philosophic about his job. She's far too intelligent to be sitting at home doing the chores. Why doesn't she get out there, take a job? Get someone else to do the housework? She'd need a car, but if a car will save our marriage she can have one tomorrow. I'll up the mortgage, and to hell with the consequences. A Chief Super's salary would help, but he'd been passed over twice . . . third time lucky, perhaps?

Automatically his thoughts returned to the case. In the morning he'd a ten-minute appointment with Sir Hubert Morrissey which Sir Charles had engineered. The Minister, said Sir Charles, had been touchy and his invective unbelievable when he learned that his conversation had been recorded. No matter that the damage done was negligible, it was the principle of the thing, attendants not doing their job, not even recognising a man in drag. Sir Charles hadn't actually criticised Sir Hubert, his litotes was admirable, but reading between the lines Byrd understood the Minister to be a man of importance, at least in his own estimation.

Stephanie was cool, oh so cool, when he arrived home.

'We'll eat at six then you can get straight off again to your band practice.'

'I thought of taking you both with me.'

'You're joking! Sit through an evening of brass in a village hall having my eardrums assaulted?'

'Oh yes, Daddy, yes please,' shouted Kate.

'It's far too late. You've got school in the morning,' said her mother sharply.

'I thought you might like to meet Jane Stormont and Kate could get to know the twins.'

Stephanie was cornered and she knew it. 'It's still too late.'

'No it isn't, Mummy.'

'Only once in a while,' he said softly.

'You can say that again!'

Detective Superintendent Byrd had left nothing to chance. He'd spoken to Dr Stormont during the day. Asked if he could leave Stephanie and Kate at the Old Rectory while the band blew the roof off the village hall. He'd made sure that Sergeant Mayhew would be in the pub after band practice. Stephanie might unwittingly pick up some threads from Jane Stormont. He needed a complete picture of her husband, a renaissance man, who could turn his hand to almost anything and succeed.

'You'll love the village, Stephie, it's one of the prettiest in the county. Ancient houses built from mellow Hornton stone. A Tudor castle, in extensive grounds, totally hidden from the road. I'm sure Jane could get permission for you both to visit the Tower, now the home of a strange lady who lives there with seven lazy cats. I gather, from Sergeant Mayhew, that she's like a character out of a children's fairy story.'

'Sergeant Mayhew! I thought she lived in Kidlington.'

'She does.'

'What's she doing in Hanwell?'

'She's working on a case.'

'So your visit tonight is business as usual?' Stephanie's voice was bleak.

'More pleasure than business,' said Byrd softly.

As he drove through the village he noticed Mayhew's car parked alongside The Little Dog Laughed. In another hundred yards they passed the post office on the left, and then the church on the right. He slowed down looking for the Old Rectory, a Georgian house of family proportions.

'There it is,' he shouted. 'It's splendid.'

'It was built in the days when the clergy sired innumerable children and had servants to look after them,' said Stephanie enviously.

He parked in the drive alongside the garages which once housed a coach and horses. As he turned off the ignition there were shouts of joy as Stephen and Sandra appeared. No introduction was necessary. They dragged Kate off to play with the dragon cars their father had made. Byrd and Stephanie took their time, breathed in the cool evening air, and slowly strolled over to the patio where Jane Stormont greeted them. She was taller than Stephanie and her hair a deeper auburn, but her eyes were the warmest, kindest eyes Byrd had seen for many moons. That was how Stephanie used to look at him. Stephanie was puzzled as she watched the cars career across the lawn.

'James, how do they work? Are they battery driven?'

'Something like that,' said Peter as he joined them. 'They are not too clever, but the children love the bright garish colour, although I think it's too crude.'

'Tonight,' said Jane, 'they have special dispensation. They can stay up until their guests leave which will give them plenty of time to play Pete's new game.'

'Come on, James, get your sax, we'll leave the children to play and the women to talk while we make music.'

By 7.30 all the players were assembled apart from Jim the postmaster who played the trombone and occasionally a flugel horn. By the time he arrived the band was singing, Why are we waiting? in raucous tones.

'Sorry chaps, Mrs Forder caught me on the doorstep, wanted her pension tonight, couldn't wait until tomorrow.'

It was a good blow. Byrd forgot his problems, both home and abroad, and concentrated on a new arrangement of Pomp and Circumstance No. 1, the opening number for the Midsummer Pageant. Stormont was good. He managed to get the best out of everyone especially the youngsters playing the cornets.

'A shade more flair needed in the opening bars,' smiling at them, 'and the tiniest smudge from the lower cornets, but you dealt with the dynamics positively. Flugel, you're slightly flat at twenty-four, and Eupho too loud.'

Stormont had literally coaxed them into giving Elgar the rounded melodious tones the piece demanded, but he was a wizard when it came to conducting *Scheherazade*.

'Good,' said Peter, 'very good, but don't forget from figure eleven . . . cheat and pick up a faster tempo. I want to hear those triplets at sixty four, and when you reach sixty-eight play it in the style of nothing, in other words let it die away.'

The Superintendent, whose lip was sore from lack of practice, was relieved when the band secretary took over and gave them instructions for the trip to Hampton Court in ten days' time. Len Smithy, a farmer from the top end of the village, looked at his notes and then peered over the top of his specs at the bandsmen.

'The coach will leave the village hall on Sunday morning at 8.30 and I mean 8.30, not 8.45, Jim Barnett, and if Mrs Forder comes for her pension you tell her what to do.'

This caused a great deal of merriment. They were all used to Jim's tardiness, and his fabulous excuses.

'With the M40 now open it should only take us an hour and a half, which means we can rehearse from ten o'clock. We've been allocated the tennis court.'

'What if it rains?' asked the euphonium.

'The tennis court is covered. It's used for real tennis, whatever that is.'

The euphonium persisted. 'The weather forecast's lousy. What happens if it's raining at two o'clock?'

'No bother,' said the farmer, 'there's a marquee.'

'Rain,' they grumbled, 'that's all we need.'

'Now the most important thing. Make sure your uniforms are presentable and clean your shoes. At our last concert there were some very mucky shoes. Remember you're on a platform. Everyone can see everything.'

'They'll not see my shoes,' yelled the percussionist.

'Why's that? Do you climb on to the platform in your stockinged feet?'

The young cornets giggled.

'You can laugh,' said Farmer Smithy, 'you were the culprits.'

'What about our families?' yelled the soprano trombone.

'There are twenty places left on the coach. Two pounds a ticket from Bill, first come, first served. The rest must make their own arrangements. Now, one thing more before we get down to the pub. Give Bill the cash for your first pint, saves Giovanni getting into a tizzy, and you get your ale without queueing.'

Byrd was ready for his pint. Giovanni, the licensee had everything timed to perfection. Nineteen pints were lined up on the counter for the men and eight cokes for the young cornet players – three girls and five boys. In seconds the bandsmen were sitting round old oak tables downing their beer as if it were nectar. As the Superintendent walked over to the corner table Sergeant Mayhew removed her handbag from the spare seat. Out of the corner of her eye she saw Peter Stormont coming their way.

'We've got company,' she mouthed.

The conductor pulled up a spare stool and joined them. Now, thought Byrd, we're stymied.

'Good evening, Georgie,' said Peter. 'Relaxing, are you, after the day's grind?'

The Superintendent stared at the pair of them in amazement. The Sergeant had been in the village barely a week, yet here she was on first-name terms with Stormont. He had to hand it to her, she was a fast worker.

'James, we'd better call you James, because we already have a Jim in the band. You don't mind, do you?' Byrd shook his head. 'James, meet Georgina who's an artist and has been making some excellent sketches of the church.'

They shook hands, Georgina, half smiling, looked him straight in the eyes.

'Tell me what you do, James.'

'I'm sure any intelligent person could guess my profession.'

She grinned. 'I'd say you worked in advertising, not as a tea-boy, but as a leader of men!'

Peter laughed. 'If a Detective Superintendent is a leader then you're half right, but you didn't quite hit the nail on the head.'

Georgina looked suitably surprised. 'I didn't think policemen had much leisure time.'

'They don't,' he snapped.

Peter couldn't quite understand the undercurrent. 'Georgina,' he said quickly, 'is a talented lady. Jane's so impressed that she's invited her to spend a week with us, do some sketches of the house . . . much more satisfactory than photographs. But you haven't given us an answer, Georgina?'

The Sergeant looked at her boss, who gave an almost imperceptible nod sanctioning the change of plan.

'I'd love to stay, but not tonight. I'll let Giovanni know I'm moving out tomorrow.'

At the far end of the bar a group of bandsmen were playing 'In the Mood'.

'Is this the usual drill?'

'It certainly is.'

'You won't mind if I don't join in. My lip's a bit sore.'

'No, of course not. Same again?' asked Peter as he rose.

'No thanks, I have to drive.'

The conductor on his way to the bar was buttonholed by the treasurer.

'Quickly, Sergeant, tell me what's going on?'

'Nothing at the moment, but yesterday over coffee, Jane let her hair down. She knows her husband's been working on a project for the MoD but she's never asked about it.'

'You've not told her who you are?'

'No, of course I haven't.' Mayhew was furious. Her boss should know her better than that.

'OK, OK, go on.'

'The first incident happened a few weeks ago. Stormont was walking in the woods with the children when two shots were fired. One shot actually went through his hat. He had the presence of mind to pull both children down on the ground. He laughed it off, said it was a poacher, but Jane thinks someone was out to get him, and seeing him fall thought the task had been completed. The next incident happened when she was working in her office, which is at the front of the house. She saw a white Cavalier hatchback drive past the house three times. The driver, she said, could have been an Arab. A little later, as she was going downstairs, she saw him standing in the churchyard looking up at the house. She was scared, rang her husband, and again he laughed it off saying that people often wandered round churchyards.'

Byrd saw that Pete was now being served. 'And the third incident, quickly?'

'She came back from shopping, on a Thursday, to be told by a neighbour that her windows had been cleaned, but her windows are always cleaned once a month on a Monday. An unknown man had arrived on a moped and had had the nerve to use a long ladder which is kept in the garage. The neighbour had seen him with a pail actually cleaning the bathroom window. Jane naturally thought there'd been a burglary. She checked everything . . . nothing missing, but the bathroom door which she'd left open was closed, and the things on the windowsill seemed too tidy. Naturally she was frightened.'

'Who's frightened?' asked Peter as he joined them.

'A friend of mine,' she said quickly, 'who's afraid of her own shadow, always imagining things, making mountains out of molehills.'

'Don't we all,' he laughed.

After the two men left, Mayhew stayed in her corner, sipping more tonic than gin, listening to the village gossip. Amazing how much one can pick up in a pub. Wouldn't be a bad idea to test the water. She wandered over to the counter and stood patiently waiting to be served.

'What is it this time, signorina?'

'Nothing more than a tonic water. I know when to stop.'

'You're a wise lass,' said the farmer at her side.

She gave him the full works. A smile which reached her eyes, slightly moist lips, her head thrown back, and a look simulating admiration.

'Aren't you the lass who's painting the church?'

'Not painting . . . just preliminary pencil sketches. The paintings come later.'

'Wouldn't mind having a picture of the old farmhouse . . . be original, wouldn't it?'

'It would be, Mr . . .'

'Len Smithy . . . call me Len.'

'Perhaps, Len, when I've finished the Stormonts' house I could take a look at the farm. But,' she bit her lip, 'there's just one small problem.'

'And what's that?'

'I've been expecting a friend . . . but he hasn't put in an appearance. We were going to take a look at Broughton Castle, but he's always having trouble with his car . . . a white Cavalier.'

'There's nothing wrong with Cavaliers, got one myself.'

'Oh, I'm sure it's not the car. It's the driver, he's as mad as a hatter.'

'White Cavalier. That's odd! I remember seeing one parked the far side of the wood, two or three weeks ago.

A hatchback it was. Bloke got a moped out and went for a ride. Made me laugh at the time, and I remember thinking . . .'

Mayhew held her breath for a moment. 'What did you think, Len?'

'Well . . . if he's your friend . . .'

'Don't worry, we're not that close.'

'Well, he could have been Greek, and they do do crazy things, don't they?'

'Greek! Oh, my friend's not Greek. Mind you, some people think he looks like an Arab.'

'Not this guy, but he could've been Italian or Maltese, take your pick.'

Mayhew laughed. 'You're certainly observant, Len.'

'You'll be coming on Sunday, won't you?' He stepped close enough to get another good whiff of her perfume.

'Well . . . well . . .'

'You must. It'll be a great day. My missis can't make it, her mother's ill, so you could have her seat, best not to waste it.'

As the two men entered the hall of the Old Rectory they heard Stephen shouting. 'I've got Sarum, I've got Sarum . . . now I'm Bishop of Salisbury.'

'Don't know why you get so excited, Stephen,' said his father.

Jane, Stephanie and the three children were sitting round a card table playing the Cathedral game. Byrd watched the child grab a card, give a whoop of delight as he read the word 'Sarum' before moving his counter on to a square depicting a church topped with a massive spire. Had to be Salisbury.

'I'm getting closer, Dad.'

'Closer to what?' asked Byrd.

'Closer to Lambeth Palace. When I get there I shall be Primate of All England, and win the game.'

'Don't be stupid,' said Sandra crossly. 'You can't win because I've got Ebor, so I'm nearer than you.'

'Uncle Paul won when he had Sarum.'

'He cheats,' said Sandra.

Jane hurried the game along. 'Get on with it, the pair of you, your guest has a long way to go.'

'I'm not going to win,' said Kate despondently.

'You will next time.'

'Can I come again? Can I, Mummy?'

'Of course, darling.'

It was a pleasant ride home. Kate asleep on the back seat, Stephanie listening to Handel's Water Music, and Byrd going through every move he'd made that day. Despite the fact that the case had stalled, it had been one of his better days. Music always caused the adrenalin to flow. Just one more thing and the day would be perfect, but it could never happen, not with Stephie in her present mood. Kate went off to bed without a murmur, and her mother decided to watch the late night arts programme. Nothing was further from Byrd's mind but he went along with it, closed his eyes and shut out the vision of ballet dancers doing the impossible, and listened to the music of Delibes. He was almost asleep when the music faded, and the voice of a man he'd not seen for a couple of years, not since he'd worked on the Tower Case, disturbed his reverie. No mistaking the clipped speech of Pierre Gambon, the Tower of London's historian, and a man whose erudition had illuminated Byrd's off-duty hours. There, in close-up, looking totally relaxed, he faced Blye German, the presenter of the programme.

'The Duke of Monmouth was a rash young man, Pierre,' said Blye smiling. A smile which reached his dark eyes. 'Would you say, therefore, that his execution was on the cards?'

'He was a tempestuous and rash young man who, with a

small army, tried to take on the might of a king and unseat him. He invited the inevitable.'

'As Historian of the Tower you must have studied Monmouth and the aftermath of Sedgemoor in depth?'

'My thesis for my degree was a treatise on Monmouth, and since taking up my appointment at the Tower I've had time to look more closely at documents relating to the case, and get the feel of the Bell Tower where he was imprisoned for twenty-four hours before his horrific end. The executioner was obviously drunk, for after five unsuccessful attempts to behead Monmouth he threw down the axe and in desperation resorted to a knife.'

'What a revolting image,' said Blye, pulling appropriate faces and taking a deep breath. 'Now that you've read the two new publications on sale this week, perhaps you'd like to share your views? The first by Robert Kettle who, a couple of years ago, wrote an excellent monograph on Bacon, and the second by Lawrence Berkeley who oddly enough, also tackled Bacon.'

Byrd, now fully awake, sat up.

'How do you rate Robert Kettle's book?'

The historian laughed derisively. 'It's an academic joke. It can only be compared with a fairy tale. Professor Kettle's tome should have been published on April 1st, not June 1st.'

James Byrd laughed until the tears ran down his face. 'You old rogue, Lawrence, you old rogue.'

Stephanie looked at him in astonishment. She hadn't heard her husband laugh like that for weeks and weeks. It was infectious. She too laughed until she cried, not knowing what she was laughing at, but it was good, very good. She moved over and sat beside him on the sofa. He put his arm round her.

'I'll explain everything in a moment, love.'

'Kettle,' continued Gambon, 'has set out to prove that Charles II married his mistress, Lucy Walters, in Belgium, and that eight years after the marriage, she arrived back in England with a seven-year-old boy, who she claimed was Charles's legitimate heir. Not surprisingly Cromwell threw her in the Tower. What he fails to say is that Lucy Walters was arrested for spying in 1656, released the same year and sent to Holland. She actually died in Paris in 1658. Kettle's hypothesis sets out to prove that there was no need for the Rebellion. All Monmouth had to do was visit Belgium, return with unassailable proof of his father's marriage, and James II, not a popular man, would, according to Kettle, have been ousted without a fight. Monmouth's legitimate birth, he argues, totally alters the line of succession. It's laughable, makes merry reading.'

'We're laughing, Lawrence, we're laughing,' said the Superintendent to the box.

Blye German smiled again, totally satisfied with the interview.

'You'd rewrite the book, would you?'

'I wouldn't put my name to it, that's a cert.'

'And Lawrence Berkeley's biography, how did that go down?'

'Sweetly. A masterpiece of scholarship, slightly underwritten, but eminently readable. It fascinated me. No romancing. Fact. Fact. Fact.'

'Thank you, Mr Gambon.'

Byrd, still chuckling to himself, switched off. 'I thought I was tired, but I'm not. That news has made my day. I'll have a cold shower while you put a bottle of champagne on ice, then we'll celebrate that crafty bastard's success, and I'll tell you a wonderful bedtime story about the downfall of a plagiarist.'

'You do that,' she said, as she ran her fingers lightly through his hair.

'Thanks, Professor,' Byrd murmured.

Sir Hubert Morrissey was decidedly prickly.

'My staff, Mr Byrd, are one hundred per cent trustworthy. No one, other than my secretary and PA would know my exact movements in detail. In my job, which is of the highest importance, prevention is my watchword. I never take papers home. They are filed here in a safe which if rifled would explode in the intruder's face, and he'd not live to tell the tale.'

'Surely, sir, you took papers to the meetings you had with Dr Stormont at Hampton Court?'

'Yes. In a bulletproof car with a chauffeur who was at one time in the SAS.'

SAS, thought Byrd. What a stroke of luck. Same mob as Abrams.

'I'm looked after, Byrd. And if you're wondering about car bombs, Simmons never leaves the car.'

'Not even for nature's call?'

'Don't be fatuous, man.'

Byrd was not put off. 'What about his meals?'

'Has them in the car. His wife, I gather, is a damn good cook.'

'And how long has Simmons been with you, Sir Hubert?'

'Two years, and I'll not change him. He's the most competent, most thoughtful chauffeur in the pool.'

'Were you aware, sir, that you were being recorded when you were perambulating in the State Apartments?'

'No, I was not and as we discussed nothing of import, I can't see that our conversation merits any further discussion. Now, if you'll excuse me, I have to leave for a meeting at the House.'

Byrd stood his ground. 'One more question, sir.'

'Go on, then, make it quick.'

'Do you remember who followed you into the Great Hall?'

'Yes, of course I do. I have a photographic memory.'

Byrd breathed out a sigh of great contentment. He was

ready to forgive the Minister his intransigence. Perhaps he deserved the job he was doing?

'We passed a woman at the top of the stairs who asked me if I wanted to hire a cassette. I told her I'd my guide with me, but one of the three people immediately behind us did stop and hire one, but the other two, oddly enough, already had theirs with them. Could have been Walkmans, of course, and they were merely listening to pop.'

'Men or women?'

'One man and two women. One of the women was very tall, almost six feet, I'd guess. After them came a family, two adults and two children, and behind them a large party of Americans.'

'Your recall is excellent, Minister. You've made my day.'

5

On a wet Sunday in June, villagers in Hanwell-on-the-Hill were up earlier than usual. They weren't too worried about the weather. Rain before seven and all that. At least they knew the outing would be pleasurable, it always was. By 8.30 the coach was full, even Jim Barnett had arrived on time. Sergeant Mayhew found herself wedged between the front-seat window and broad-beamed Farmer Smithy with scarcely enough room to breathe, but she too was going to enjoy the outing, come what may. Jane Stormont sat behind with Sandra, and Peter, across the gangway, with Stephen. The children had spent many holidays with their grandmother at the palace, always travelling by car; a coach was much more fun.

The driver left the village as the church clock struck the half hour, and seven minutes later eased his way on to the M40. By the time he passed the Oxford exit the bandsmen and camp followers were in good voice. She'll be Coming Round the Mountain, followed by Nine Green Bottles and Men of Harlech for Taffy Jones the trumpet. The only musician missing from this riotous assembly was the bearded saxophonist who'd left Bletchingdon at 7.30 with his family.

Shortly before ten o'clock Peter Stormont instructed the driver to stop for a few minutes alongside the magnificent Lion Gate, a memorial, so Lady Stormont had once written, to the parsimony and unreliability of princes.

'In an attempt to outshine Versailles,' Peter told his

captive audience, 'William III commissioned Jean Tijou to design the entrance, but after Tijou had paid for all the materials and built the massive stone piers William decided to cut costs and have small iron gates fitted. Poor Tijou was never fully recompensed, in fact he was threatened with a debtors' prison, and the saddened Frenchman, who'd put his trust in princes, returned to France with a pittance.'

As Sergeant Mayhew turned her head to get a better look at the lions atop the piers she saw Peter unscrew a small bottle, shake a couple of pills into his hand and swallow them. Why can't I do that? she wondered. Why do I always need water?

The coach then continued on to the Trophy Gate where a lion and a unicorn, not fighting any more, stood proudly supporting shields bearing the arms of George II.

The driver, following instructions from a security guard, drove through the gates and parked the coach on the forecourt below the Administration Block. Camp followers and bandsmen carrying their instruments and maroon jackets disembarked while the driver rushed to open the hold where the percussion kit was stowed. A warder, miraculously, appeared with a trolley which was trundled along to Henry VIII's tennis court.

The torrential rain had dwindled to a drizzle, but the sky remained a dismally depressing grey. A few rushed off to experience the maze and its wondrous convolutions, some to see the Great Vine, some to the State Apartments and Jane Stormont, who left the twins in Mrs Barnett's care, joined her mother-in-law for the 11 a.m. Choral Eucharist in the Chapel Royal.

Byrd, on his arrival earlier, had gone straight to the Incident Room leaving Stephanie and Kate to wander at will until 11.30 when they planned to meet up in the coffee shop. The phlegmatic and unemotional Mozart looked up at Byrd with something resembling excitement written all over his face.

'What is it, Inspector?'

'We've found the missing shoe.'

'Where?'

'In the undergrowth near the car park. Gardener came across it when he was weeding.'

'Good. One more bit of the jigsaw.'

'Why didn't they take it with them?'

'In case they were stopped, perhaps? A clean car with nothing in it to connect them with the murder. The same reason, Wolfgang, our tall friend jettisoned the wig in the Ladies' loo.'

Mozart looked up in surprise. Christian-name terms! What was clever boots after now?

'You interviewed the warder who was on duty in the Royal Pew on the afternoon of the murder, didn't you?'

'Yes, sir.' Emphasis on the 'sir' which Byrd didn't miss.

'Have you your notes to hand?'

'Yes.'

'Go through them, will you. Read out everything the man said.'

The Inspector took his time.

'Boyle's the man's name. Mike Boyle. "I came on duty at two o'clock. Business was slow until 2.20 when a group from a Women's Institute up north arrived. There were thirty of them so they had the services of an official guide. They spent about fifteen minutes looking at the Chapel from the Royal Pew. Shortly afterwards another group arrived. This time from a comprehensive school in Milton Keynes. The teacher knew what he was about but the kids looked tired. Probably tried to see too much. At about five past three half a dozen Japanese came in followed by another two or three people who were on their own. At this time all areas on both left and right of the Royal Pew were open. The Japanese were standing on the left looking up at the ceiling while one of their number gave them the history. I couldn't understand what he was saying, of course, but they were very attentive until one of them took out a camera and started taking flash photos. I stopped it at once. We had quite an argument, but I was quite firm, not rude you understand, but after their leader had finished bowing and apologising they went on their . . ."

'That's it, sir, that's it . . . while the warder's attention was diverted the doors to the ante-room were closed.'

'You're right,' said Byrd, annoyed that the evidence which was crystal clear hadn't been picked up before. 'Only needed a few seconds. The argument with the warder would have covered any noise Sarah Jackson made. First the injection which may not have taken immediate effect, and then the plastic bag over her head to make sure. While the contretemps with the Japanese was still going on the murderer opened the door nearest to the exit, closed it again and made his escape.'

'And then, sir, went to the loo and divested himself of the wig?'

'No, I think not. He'd done that earlier. Mrs Jackson was in one of the cubicles when he entered. He locked the main door which is on a yale, and removed the wig but at that very moment she emerged from her cubicle, saw what he was doing, and possibly remonstrated with him. He may have laughed it off, but when she left and went up the Queen's Stairs, against the flow of traffic, he followed her.'

'Had it occurred to you, sir, that Dr Jackson, who was sitting on the bench in the Haunted Gallery probably saw the murderer leave? He's the only person who knows what the man actually looks like minus his wig.'

'Yes. I came to that conclusion and thought we'd keep him on ice until we find the bastard. He's safe enough in New Jersey.'

'Well I'm damned!'

'Now what, Inspector?'

'I'm not clairvoyant, sir. Isn't it about time you occasionally shared your thoughts? Might do a little towards solving a case which is now stalemate.'

Byrd looked at the older man, who'd not much longer to go, recognised too that seventeen days of unspoken criticism had at last boiled over. It was his own fault . . . the way he always worked . . . saw too many possibilities . . . dreamt up too many scenarios . . . sometimes off beam . . . steered clear of ridicule by keeping ideas close to his chest . . . but with lateral thinking he usually managed to reach the tape well ahead of the field.

'Inspector . . .' he said at last.

'I'm sorry, sir, forget what I've just said.'

'No, I can't forget. You're right. I hesitate to share . . . could send out the wrong signals. Sometimes a case is like trying to solve an easy crossword, which is often more difficult than an abstruse puzzle, because there are too many alternatives, get one answer wrong and you've buggered up the rest. Now if it were a difficult crossword like Ximenes there'd be only one answer, but if you want the truth, I hesitate to make predictions, wrong diagnoses can rebound . . . there'd be egg . . .'

'Yes, yes I can see that.'

'You might, Inspector, spend the rest of the morning on the computer . . . read through everything Charlie spews up . . . see if you can find a reference to a white Cavalier hatchback.'

'Was that their car?'

'May have been . . . could be another esoteric fancy . . . it's been seen twice in Hanwell-on-the-Hill, once by Mrs Stormont who later saw the driver taking an interest in her house, and again by Farmer Smithy who noticed a young man park a car on the edge of Witchwood, unload a moped and ride off. Jane Stormont thought the driver looked like an Arab, and Smithy, though some distance away, plumped for a Mediterranean type.'

'Back to our Cypriots.'

'Yes.'

Wolfgang thought about the car for some time. 'I can't fathom, sir, what a car in Hanwell has to do with two murders in the palace.'

'A gut feeling, that's all it is, because I'm certain everything in this case revolves round Peter Stormont.'

'Sergeant Mayhew hasn't stumbled on anything, has she?'

'An attempted murder, possibly, and an intruder who stole nothing.'

Mozart couldn't believe his ears. In five minutes this impossible man had produced facts which he was damn certain hadn't been recorded.

'This intruder, presumably, was looking for something specific?'

'Must have been, but he was on a losing wicket if he was searching for the recent MoD plans. They were kept in Lady Stormont's safe and have now been removed to the War Office.'

'Do I take it then that the white Cavalier has disappeared and everything has returned to normal in Hanwell?'

'Yes,' sighed Byrd. 'A difficult case . . . can't see a way through the maze . . . my head on the block . . .'

That's where it ought to be, thought Mozart, as Byrd went off to his band rehearsal leaving behind a more cheerful inspector, who despite his hatred of modern technology and Charlie's idiosyncrasies sat down at the keyboard to have a go.

The reverberation in the real-tennis court produced an extraordinarily uneven sound, but the conductor wasn't too bothered. He knew as he concentrated on Pomp and Circumstance for the benefit of the saxophonist, who'd only managed two band practices, that it would sound fifty times better in the open air. Len Smithy noted, with satisfaction, that the cornets had actually used a bit of spit and polish on their shoes; not only that, but their white shirts were pristine, their maroon velvet bow ties reasonably straight, and their black trousers, which the lasses were also wearing, were passable. At a moment when the band was playing fortissimo he caught a glimpse of Stephanie and Kate sneaking into the pavilion. They remained hidden in the shadows under the canopy which covered the entire side of the court.

'I don't believe Henry VIII played tennis, Mummy.'

'Why's that?'

'He was too fat to run about.'

'Not when he was a young man. He was quite athletic.'

'Did he chop the heads off, or did someone do it for him?'

Stephanie didn't answer, she was staring at her husband who was concentrating on his score. He looked tired. She knew he'd not been sleeping, this case had got to him, he'd even murmured 'unsolvable' in his sleep. What had happened? He was normally so ebullient, so confident. She castigated herself for being stupid, for seeing that moronic young solicitor who'd sat there grinning inanely waiting for her to go through chapter and verse about her failing marriage. He'd had the temerity to ask about their sexual relationship intimating that it always had a bearing in divorce cases. 'Is that how you get your kicks?' she'd asked angrily and stormed out of his office.

The informal lunch laid on by Lady Stormont in her Grace and Favour apartment was fun especially for the children. They were given their own table in the kitchen and allowed to help themselves from a superb cold buffet. Coke for them, but a light hock for their parents.

After lunch, Byrd donned Pete's maroon jacket. It wasn't too bad a fit. A little short in the sleeves, maybe, but who would notice? Pete looked splendid in a blue velvet smoking-jacket which his mother had given him the previous Christmas.

'What a pity, Peter, you didn't go in for music professionally.'

'So that you could go to a concert every day of the week, eh Mother?'

'No, dear. Twice a week would suffice.'

Jane gazed through the drawing-room windows at the crowds already assembling, thinking they should be wearing summer dresses and straw hats, not wearing macs and carrying umbrellas.'

'Look Nana,' shouted Sandra, 'there's a bit of blue sky.'

'Not enough to make a pair of sailor's bell bottoms.'

'It will be big enough in a minute. Look!'

The child was right. Within half an hour the dark clouds drifted slowly east leaving a clear blue sky. Lady Stormont was thrilled.

'This is what I've prayed for, Peter. Sunshine, music, and crowds of happy people. Our Midsummer Pageant will be something to remember.'

They all laughed. Her enthusiasm was infectious.

Ten minutes later, when the percussionist had set up all his paraphernalia and the audience was sitting comfortably, the bandsmen assembled on the platform. Lady Stormont, Jane and Stephanie sat on the second row with the three children in front of them. The Colonel and his wife settled themselves on back row seats twelve rows away from the stage. Abrams, who'd arranged for 150 seats to be set up, wished he'd catered for more people, but with this damned weather you never knew where you were. The last two seats on the back row were taken by a couple in their mid thirties. The woman was wearing a brilliant orange and purple headscarf which clashed with the red dress she was wearing. She didn't look too pleased, making quite a fuss because she wanted to be nearer to the stage. Ah well, they should have arrived earlier.

He stood chatting to Wolfgang who'd spent three hours giving Charlie a hard time although his efforts produced nothing. He needed a little light relief, the concert was just the job.

At two o'clock precisely the audience applauded as Peter climbed up the six steps on to the platform. A youthful, debonair and handsome conductor faced the audience, bowed and winked at his mother before turning to face the band. He stood waiting patiently for them to settle. The alto sax and trumpet were still emptying their instruments of excess fluid before finding the right pitch. The metamorphosis from a dull dismal day into a hot bright June afternoon was miraculous. Lady Stormont sat there glowing. The committee had done a grand job. If it worked this year they'd make it an annual event. There was plenty for the public to see and do, Morris dancers, clowns, short river trips, children's bouncy castle, Nell Gwyn lookalikes, tumblers, stalls galore, and after the brass band had finished there'd be madrigals in Fountain Court, followed by a celestial choir in the Chapel during the evening, and fireworks to round off a wonderful day. Yes, the committee had done well.

James Byrd, who had not played in public for two years, was feeling quite nervous. He should have practised more, but there was never enough time, that was the story of his life. He found the heat oppressive, and thought how much better off they'd be sitting in an old-fashioned bandstand protected from the relentless sun. The bandsmen sat patiently awaiting the conductor's smile followed by a slight nod, always the same ritual. The saxophonist, waiting for the upbeat, kept his eyes on the conductor, and was surprised to see him sweating. Peter took a handkerchief out of his left hand pocket and wiped his forehead. Funny to think of him being nervous, he's done this sort of thing so often. Jim Barnett coughed, clearing his throat, which he always did; the percussionist, looking as though he had the troubles of the world on his shoulders, was worrying about his girlfriend who'd told him on the way down that she was preggers; Len Smithy fidgeted, the damned seat was far too small to accommodate his backside; Taffy wondered why the conductor didn't get going, they'd never waited this long before. The audience was chatting again, not a good sign, but what the hell was Pete thinking about? Neither Taffy nor anyone else was prepared for what happened next. Pete reeled slightly, dropping his baton, then he grabbed the solid music stand which rocked precariously. The audience was shocked into silence, and the bandsmen rooted to their seats. The distant sound of a plane on its way to Heathrow faded, and in those few seconds of silence the band and spectators in the front row could hear the conductor's laboured breathing. He twisted slightly, and the astonished audience watched as his face swelled visibly. Afterwards Abrams said that everyone was mesmerised. Too bizarre to believe. In seconds his lips were so swollen they reached his nose, and his eyes, no longer visible, looked like puffballs. The change happened with such speed that it hardly seemed real. His hands became puffed and the collar round his swollen neck so tight that it could easily have strangled him. Then the convulsions started. Byrd was the first to move. He caught Pete as he collapsed. Sandra and Stephen ran to the front of the stage screaming while Jane ran up the steps and knelt beside her husband who was now supine on the floor. The children tried to follow Jane, but Lady Stormont managed to hang on to them though nothing she could do would calm them. Stephanie grabbed Kate who attempted to follow them. Jim Barnett was hysterical, and his wife in the audience even worse, thinking the shock would bring on one of Jim's epileptic fits. Two of the frightened young cornets cried and hugged each other while the rest of the band crowded round their conductor until Len told them in no uncertain terms to sit down. Byrd removed Pete's bow tie, unbuttoned his shirt, and placed the borrowed jacket under his head. Colonel Wishart was having words with Abrams who'd already asked the Royal Parks Police to send a stretcher before handing his phone to Mozart who rang for an ambulance and police escort. Dr Kelsoe, who'd been on the fringe waiting for the concert to begin, thrust his way through the noisy crowd and leapt on to the stage.

'Superintendent, I'll need my bag from the car.'

'OK. Give me your keys. What sort of car, where's it parked and the number?'

'Red Montego, O registration, opposite the police office in reserved parking.'

'I'll get it, sir,' said Mozart who was standing on the ground in front of the stage. Anything to escape.

Kelsoe took one look at the unconscious man and decided not to move him until the stretcher arrived. All he could do was borrow an umbrella from someone in the crowd to keep the sun off the unconscious man's face. By the time Abrams had unlocked the doors of the Conservation Office and opened up the library two policemen arrived with a stretcher.

Inside the small library it was blessedly cool, but no provision for a sick man. Tom Abrams improvised hastily, clearing two tables of books and papers, pushing them together to form a makeshift bed before removing the velvet door curtain which he folded and laid over the tables. In the next room he found a cushion on the typist's chair to serve as a pillow. The two attendants lifted Peter Stormont gently on to the stretcher, and led a slow procession including Jane, the twins, Lady Stormont, Mozart and Dr Kelsoe into the library where Abrams was waiting.

Len Smithy caught Byrd before he had time to move. 'What are we going to do, James?'

'Give a concert, of course.'

'What! You're not suggesting that we go on as if . . .'

'That's what Dr Stormont would have expected. You can conduct, can't you?'

'Never done it in public.'

'Well, here's your chance. Get on with it. Pull them together.'

'I suppose you're right,' said Len miserably.

Byrd reached the library as the unconscious man was being transferred from the stretcher on to the table.

'Gently does it,' said Kelsoe. As the doctor took his stethoscope out he whispered to Lady Stormont, asking her to take the children into the next room. Stephen heard every word.

'I'm not going,' he shouted. 'I'm staying with Mummy.'

'I want to examine your dad,' said the doctor softly.

'I'm not going.'

'It's all right,' said Jane, 'leave him.'

Lady Stormont put her arm round Sandra, who was sobbing her heart out, and withdrew. She sat with the child on an outside wall wondering what had happened to a day which had begun so full of promise. What was wrong with Peter? He'd never suffered a heart condition. As strong as an ox, she'd been led to believe. His diabetes had really been no problem as long as he took Tolbutamide regularly. She sighed. Had he been overworking? Hypertension. Was that what it was all about?

Dr Kelsoe shook his head knowing this was outside his experience. He'd never seen a man blow up in front of his eyes. It was grotesque. Had to be an allergy, but caused by what?

'Has he eaten any shellfish recently, Mrs Stormont?'

'No. Is it food poisoning?'

'I don't know. If it is, it's the most virulent I've ever seen.'

He thought back to the years when he was a student, remembered reading a vast tome on 'Toxins and Their

Effects' in which the writer stated that the African hornet could cause swelling in a matter of seconds.

'The African hornet,' he murmured, 'here in the palace gardens? Not possible.'

Jane tried to catch what he was saying. 'Never seen the results, only read about them, you understand.'

What was he talking about? She was lost.

'Is he on antihistamine?'

'No, but he takes Tolbutamide.'

'Does he now? That may account for it. Most of these anti-diabetic drugs produce photosensitisation which is a side effect. Could have taken an overdose.'

'I doubt it. It's usually the other way round. He forgets.'

'Then what happens?'

'He has difficulty in breathing.'

'Like now?'

'No, never as bad as this,' said Jane, gritting her teeth determined not to cry.

Abrams' phone bleeped. 'Yes?'

'Ambulance on its way, sir.'

'How long?'

'Less than ten minutes, sir.'

Kelsoe was muttering to himself, 'Breath sweet . . . odd . . . toxic substance . . . diabetic . . . systemic . . .'

'Mrs Stormont,' asked Byrd, another of his inspired ideas surfacing. 'What's your husband experimenting on at the moment?'

'Nothing, as far as I know.'

'Yes he is, Mummy. He's trying to get the dynamics right on our dragon cars.'

'Yes, darling, but that's not what Mr Byrd meant.'

Jane looked down on her husband. No, not her husband. A shape she didn't recognise, a body with a strange sickly smell washed up by the sea. Bloated. Unrecognisable.

Dr Kelsoe's expression as he used his stethoscope said it all.

Tom Abrams whispered, 'Five minutes.'

The doctor nodded.

'What's he doing, Mummy?'

'Shush, he's listening to Daddy's heart.'

There was an awful stillness in the room, so still they could hear the band playing Scheherazade. At that moment Pete's arm flopped down by the side of the table.

In a split second Kelsoe had thrown off his jacket, ripped the patient's vest off and was massaging his heart. After some minutes he shook his head and bent over the now lifeless body and tried mouth to mouth resuscitation all to no effect.

'I'm afraid,' said Dr Kelsoe quietly, 'he's gone.'

Byrd looked at Jane. She seemed to die too. She closed her eyes and stood like a statue, motionless, apart.

Stephen screamed and grabbed his father's arm. 'Daddy, Daddy, you're not going to die. I won't let you.' He kept hold of his father's arm, closed his eyes, as if by closing them he could blot out the image.

'Laddie, laddie,' said the doctor, prising him away from his father. 'You are going to be a brave man. You've got to look after your mother now. How old are you?'

'Nine,' he sobbed.

'That's old enough.'

Mozart, who abhorred emotional scenes, whether it was on screen or in life, made himself scarce. He couldn't bear the grief nor the love which the family had for the sick man. He'd never been that close to anyone. Never loved anyone other than his parents, an undemonstrative love. Neither he nor his father shed a tear when his mother died, the spring too tight . . . impossible to release, but they talked to her and about her as though she were still alive.

He'd never wanted nor needed male or female companionship, he was solitary, self-sufficient, undemanding. Undemanding, too, in his job, but despite being an unambitious man he bore a grudge, a deep-seated antipathy to those graduates who went through police college and arrived knowing all the answers, bucking the system and taking the piss out of regular down-to-earth coppers. The afternoon's events had proved the bearded bastard right. Stormont was the catalyst, but if his death happened to be a most unnatural death which would bring clouds of wrath down upon the head of Byrd, so be it. Two murders had remained unsolved for seventeen days. What price a third? He settled himself down in front of Charlie and diligently fed him with cordon bleu information.

While Mozart was hammering away at the keys, the body of Dr Peter Stormont was placed in the ambulance. Colonel Wishart joined the sad family group already mourning the death of a son, a husband and a father. Lady Stormont, who'd worked so hard to make the Pageant a success, never dreamt that her son whom the audience had applauded, her son who'd smiled at them would in less than half an hour be unrecognisable . . . dead from a massive heart attack.

Tom Abrams, who'd persuaded Jane to remain with her mother-in-law, climbed into the ambulance. He was hardened to death, but not this kind of death, death on a sunny afternoon in an English garden. He'd seen many men die in action, and as an observer he'd seen nerve gas backfire on those who were dispensing it with horrendous consequences, but he'd never seen anyone die as Dr Stormont had died. A nightmarish death that even Hitchcock could never have envisaged. The ambulance left the palace silently, no klaxon blaring, no light flashing, travelling at a funereal pace.

Sergeant Mayhew, at a nod from Byrd, shepherded

Lady Stormont, her daughter-in-law and grandchildren back to the apartment.

Stephanie, who'd watched events from a distance, realised Pete was dead. She felt she ought to help, but she couldn't face the agony, neither could she expose Kate to such utter misery. Kate who would crash in, asking interminable questions. Or would she? Was she making excuses, finding a way out? She felt guilty, but death was something she'd never faced. Supposing, she thought, it had been James? She could see him sitting on the platform in Pete's maroon jacket, his eyes firmly fixed on the conductor. He'd been looking forward to the outing, a break from the strain of the past two and a half weeks, but supposing he'd collapsed, he was much the same age as Peter, supposing . . . he'd died?

'Why are you crying, Mummy?'

'For us all, darling.'

Kate looked puzzled. 'Can I have an ice cream, Mummy?'

'Yes. We'll walk down to the river, get one on the way.'

Colonel Wishart joined Kelsoe and Byrd in the library listening while the policeman tried to pin the doctor down to a considered diagnosis. The doctor knew what lay behind the questions. He was chary, went slowly, too much the medical profession didn't know, the effects of toxin still not fully understood.

'Toxin!' Wishart was shaken. 'Are you saying it was not a heart attack?'

'That's exactly what I'm saying. Poison, Colonel, was the cause, but remember in poison there is physic. Who's to say he didn't take amphetamines to give himself a boost for the concert? I'm neither a pathologist nor a chemist, nor do I know what effect amphetamines would have if taken on top of Tolbutamide.'

'He was an intelligent man,' said Byrd. 'A chemist and

a scientist, I can't see him chancing his arm. Tell me, off the record, what do you really think?'

'A systemic poison.' Kelsoe chose his words carefully. 'A poison that can kill with a lightning rapidity, something like hydrocyanic acid, in other words, cyanide. A favourite method used by the Nazi war criminals. Himmler bit into a glass capsule and swallowed the contents, and Goering had it smuggled into his cell in a tobacco pipe. Efficacious because the poison is readily absorbed into the stomach, diffuses through circulation and produces symptoms in seconds, not minutes.'

'In that case, doctor, how did he make it from the apartment to the platform?'

'On rare occasions victims have been known to act normally, but only for a few minutes, before symptoms develop. First breathing is impaired, followed by a slow heart action, and convulsions accompanied by an overwhelming smell of bitter almonds. I have also seen a fine froth round the mouth and irregular pink patches on the face and body, but never the type of swelling we've just seen.'

'But there was a distinctive smell, a sweet smell,' persisted Byrd.

'Yes, I agree, but it was not the same. Now if you'll excuse me, I'll see what can be done for the ladies.'

'He's a good fellow,' said the Colonel, as they watched him bustle off. 'A great support to many of the residents here. You could say he was here at the right place . . .'

'But not at the right time, sir, for Dr Stormont,' said Byrd grimly.

'I can't believe that a young man with everything to live for committed suicide. It had to be accidental.'

'It was not suicide and it was not accidental.'

'What! Another murder? Aren't you jumping the gun, Mr Byrd? Hadn't we better wait for the result of the autopsy?'

'You can wait, sir, but I guarantee there'll be all hell let loose tomorrow. Sir Elwyn will be down here demanding action, and wanting to know how a man was killed in such a public place in full view. *How*, Colonel, is the most important question. I sat on the platform watching him closely, never took my eyes off him. No one was near him, no dart was fired, unless it happened as he walked across the lawn.'

'No dart! You thinking about curare?'

'I can think of no other way of killing a man so quickly and effectively. It couldn't be what he ate because we all ate the same food, we drank the same wine, we poured from the same coffee jug. There were no strangers there, no one to slip a capsule into his food or drink.'

They heard the applause, the shouts of 'Encore', 'Well done', and 'Bravo', as the band played the final chords of the Slaves Chorus from *Nabucco*. Ironic, thought Byrd, Pete's favourite tune became his final tribute, triumph only for the assassin who'd done it again . . . but I'll get you, you bastard. Now the unpleasant task of breaking it to the band.

'I'd better get out there, sir. They won't be giving an encore.'

The Colonel nodded. 'I'll get back to my office and wait for Tom Abrams. Madrigals, a celebration in the Chapel, and fireworks seem out of place, but they can't be cancelled. Too many people have come too far. Like they say in the theatre, the show must go on.'

Dr Patel, the young pathologist on duty in the Path lab grinned at Abrams as he entered. 'Making a habit of this, are you, Captain? Keeping the place in the news? Three corpses now, in three weeks, a hat trick you could say, on a par with Jack the Ripper.'

'Cut the crap and get moving. We need an opinion, pronto. The official report can follow tomorrow.'

'Oh, I don't know about that. I'm suffering from writer's cramp.'

'Which hasn't prevented you, I see, from doing the *Observer* crossword.'

'It's not finished, but like everything else I do, it has to be solved. You're an army man, think about thirteen down. "A naval action is never thinly disguised by an eleven." Nine letters.'

'Broadside,' he snapped. 'Now can we get on with the job?'

Dr Patel nodded to the technicians. They lifted the body on to the mortuary table, switched on the overhead light, removed the dead man's clothes, and covered him with a sheet which Abrams whipped straight off, keeping his eyes on the pathologist. Patel stood and stared in disbelief at the bloated oedematous mass on the table. He was stunned.

'My God, what a mess . . . should have been brought in hours ago, they may have been able to save him.'

'No chance. It happened at two o'clock. Came up in a few seconds, like a balloon.'

'What's he been eating?'

'The same as everyone else. It happened in full view of the audience.'

'Audience!'

'He was about to conduct an open-air concert in the palace grounds. He bowed to the audience, and as he turned to face the band this happened.'

The doctor sniffed. 'Definitely not cyanide, prussic acid or arsenic. A sweet smell, deodorant, I'd say.'

'How long is it going to take you?'

'An hour, two hours, who can tell? Why don't you have a coffee in the staff canteen, and take the crossword with you?'

He turned his back on Abrams and took a closer look at the corpse. 'An interesting case. Never tackled anything like this before.'

'Don't you ever get sick of it?'

'No, Captain, like I said, I like solving things.'

The audience slowly dispersed, disappointed at being deprived of an encore, but there were many other diversions.

Len Smithy saw the Superintendent making his way over, knew from his measured tread, the hang of the head, that the news was bad. The cornets, who were gasping for a drink, were impatient to get moving.

'Wait folks, wait. Let's hear what James has to say.'

It wasn't easy. They listened but didn't speak. He felt like a prophet of doom, the Greeks gazing at him accusingly. Cries of children shouting at Mr Punch stopped him in mid flow. He moistened his lips and carried on. Apologised, said he was sorry that Pete was dead. Sorry that it had happened like this.

Why hadn't he prevented it? He'd known, but how had he known? Why was he so sure? Something Mayhew had said, was that it? But what? She must get back to the village, take her place on the coach with the bandsmen, stay at the Old Rectory, any explanation would do. The answer was there. Had to be. None of the bandsmen nor their families wanted to join in the festivities. They couldn't celebrate. Not now.

Jane Stormont opened the door. He looked at her in amazement. Not a hair out of place, her brilliant emerald-green dress accentuating her pale skin, even a wan smile. She looked down at the jacket he was carrying.

'You keep it, James. One of these days, perhaps, you'll play for us again.'

It was the shock. Hadn't struck home yet. Almost as if she'd blotted out the events of the afternoon, her way of coping.

'Don't stand there, James, come in, have a cup of tea.'

'I thought Stephanie and Kate might be here.' He realised with a sick feeling in his stomach that it was far from the truth. He'd not given them a thought since it happened. Where were they, he wondered?

Dr Kelsoe and Lady Stormont were discussing one of the previous occupants who'd lived in her apartment. An amazing lady, descended from Elizabeth Fry, who'd lost her husband during the war. He'd been killed with the Duke of Kent when their Sunderland flying boat crashed somewhere in Scotland. She'd had a fighting spirit and an enquiring mind, and lived to a ripe old age.

How strange, thought Byrd, that Lady Stormont is harping on a death in the past, but avoiding the present. She took his arm.

'It's good of you, Mr Byrd, to be with us, Dr Kelsoe too, although the doctor is here with an ulterior motive. He thinks we're going to take knock-out pills, but neither Jane nor I wish to be sedated. We've the children to think about.'

'Where are the children?'

'Sandra's asleep, poor lamb, totally exhausted. Stephen's in the study with Georgina playing one of those mind-boggling computer games. Good for him, keeps his mind off things.'

'Will they stay on with you?' asked Byrd tentatively.

'For a couple of days, no more,' said Jane as she entered the room.

'But Jane . . .'

'No Mother, we're going home, normality is what the children need. School as usual, their own beds.'

Not as normal, thought the doctor, but kept his counsel. The telephone rang. They all looked at it, wondering. Could be Abrams, thought Byrd. Jane hesitated before picking it up. He saw her look of amazement. What now?

'Good God,' said Jane. 'Malta! you're ringing from

Malta, you really are a gadabout. What are you doing there? It's Paul,' she whispered. 'I'm sorry, Paul, but you can't speak to Peter, he . . . he died this afternoon.' Her voice trembled. 'We don't know yet . . . could have been food poisoning . . . could have . . .' She took a deep breath. 'Yes, we're staying with Mother for a couple of days. What! No, no, I'd rather they stayed with me, very kind of you. I appreciate the thought. Goodbye Paul, goodbye . . .'

She put the phone down. 'Paul wanted Anthea to collect the twins and take them down to the houseboat at Abingdon, but I need them with me.'

'You're quite right, my dear, this is a family business,' said Lady Stormont, who'd never taken to Anthea and Paul despite what they'd done for Peter.

'Who is Paul?' asked Dr Kelsoe. Anything to divert their minds.

'You explain, Mother.'

'He's an old friend of Peter's. His tutor, at one time, but he gave up his Chair at Cambridge to become a big noise. He likes a bit of clout, does Paul.' Byrd sensed the disapproval. 'He's the chairman now of a large oil company. Jets his way around the world, but to give him his due he does remember his godchildren.'

Jane interrupted. 'They've always been allowed to play on the houseboat, a narrowboat really, they cook their own meals, wash up and play mothers and fathers . . .'

Tears coursed down her cheeks. 'Excuse me, I'll see how Stephen's getting on.'

James Byrd followed her into the hall. Eventually she'd have to be told why Georgina was in Hanwell, but not for the moment, leave it a few days.

'This computer game, I gather, is a brain stretcher. Is Stephen good at it?'

'Yes, he'll run rings round Georgina, she won't get a look-in.'

As they went into the study Mayhew looked at him, her vivid eyes asking for instructions. That look, he thought, could easily turn a man's blood to water.

'Len Smithy asked me to tell you that the coach will be returning to Hanwell in ten minutes. "Don't be late" were his last words.'

'Thank you, James.' She acted out the charade to perfection. 'I'd better get back there, collect my stuff, and get from under Jane's feet.'

'There's no need to leave, Georgina, you stay until you've had enough of us, though you might find things a little strained.'

Byrd nodded. He didn't have to, she knew exactly what was in his mind.

'I'd like to stay, Jane, and keep an eye on the place until you get back.'

'Aren't we going to finish?' asked Stephen crossly.

'You've won, Stephen, or you will in two more moves. We'll have another game when you get home.'

The child said nothing. He looked at the faces of the adults, and then burst into tears.

Stephanie sat on the bank thinking about the literature which had arrived the previous day. She'd not discussed it with James, there was never enough time, even less now. She fancied the legal course proposed by the Open Collegiate. It opened all sorts of doors. She had two 'A' levels which meant she needn't bother with a foundation course. Four years it would take. They'd also suggested biochemistry, but that might not prove as useful as law. If she could get the job she'd seen advertised by Sprott & Salisbury in the *Oxford Mail* she'd be well on her way. 'Part time receptionist required in Solicitors' Office. 9 a.m. to 1 p.m. four days a week.' That would suit her down to the ground.

Kate had finished her ice cream and was getting fidgety. The child was agog to go on the water.

'All right, darling, we'll take a short trip up the river as far as Sunbury and back.'

'Will Daddy come with us?'

'He's busy, darling, he has a lot of problems.'

Hubert Morrissey, who never spent his weekends in the Great Wen, was sipping a Tio Pepe in his hideaway in West Sussex when his wife turned on the six o'clock news.

'Do we want to hear it, Dora? We've heard the nine o'clock, and the one o'clock. Isn't that enough? I come down here for peace.'

'All right, Hughie, just the headlines.' Lady Morrissey was a practised placator. It was the same again, a plane crash in Chile, an earthquake of horrendous proportions in Japan, another murder in Northern Ireland, an unexpected Test win for England, Mansell in pole position, and the Prime Minister making another of his anti-European speeches. The same again except for the last newsflash.

'Today's celebrations at Hampton Court Palace were marred when Dr Peter Stormont who was about to conduct a brass band concert collapsed on the platform.'

'What!' yelled Sir Hubert leaping out of his seat.

The announcer carried on without inflexion. 'He died half an hour later without having recovered consciousness.'

'I'm off, Dora. Don't wait dinner for me.'

'Where on earth are you going?'

'To see Elwyn, now.'

'But it has nothing to do with you,' wishing she'd never turned the damn box on.

'It has everything to do with me. That's why that CID man was asking so many questions.'

'I don't know what you're talking about.'

'No, no, of course you don't. I'll explain later.'

She smiled wryly. She knew he never would.

6

The young pathologist wasn't sure. He'd spent three and a half hours making all the usual tests. Nothing was going right, even the incisions weren't up to his normal standard, he could do better than that, but the flabbiness caused by the swelling had made precision impossible. Liver, kidney, urine and stomach content had all been tested. There were very few traces of the daily intake of Tolbutamide, itself a sulphonamide derivative which could produce a mild state of photosensitisation, but there was an excess of porphyrin. What, he wondered, would the chemical reaction of porphyrin be in a deranged metabolism? It was worth exploring.

After the river trip up to Sunbury and back Stephanie decided to look for her husband. She had a minor contretemps with the guard at the barrier in Tennis Court Lane before being allowed in and directed to the Incident Room. Much to Byrd's surprise she accepted the situation with equanimity. She would take the car, drive back as he suggested, and wouldn't expect him home for at least a couple of days. She took a look at the guest room, tested the bed and murmured her approval.

During the three hours following Pete's death she'd come to terms with life in Bletchingdon alongside an ambitious superintendent. She couldn't change him, she didn't want to change him. He was alive not lying on a slab, better a small part of him than nothing. A bleak dreary nothing.

By the time she and Kate drove out of the palace gates the coach carrying Sergeant Mayhew and the bandsmen had arrived back in Hanwell-on-the-Hill. Georgina refused Len's offer of a quick drink at The Little Dog Laughed knowing there'd be nothing quick about it.

She let herself into the house, made a cup of tea, then set about following the instructions Byrd had whispered as she left the apartment. 'Don't leave a stone unturned,' he'd said. She tackled the study first. After she'd been through every drawer in the desk she systematically set about removing and checking every book in the Chippendale bookcase. No loose sheets, nothing stuck in between the end pages, nothing written in the margins. The briefcase under the desk was locked, but she managed to prise it open with a penknife. It yielded nothing of import, neither did the box files.

Disappointed she made herself another cup of tea, sat down at the desk, and idly thumbed through the leaflets in the box files which had been published by the Open Collegiate in Milton Magnus. She was fascinated. They introduced her to photosynthesis, a subject about which she knew absolutely nothing. On the bottom of the pile were four leaflets written by Paul Burgess in 1982, the man who'd phoned from Malta. It was chance, pure chance that she knew who he was, chance that she'd decided to answer the phone, and had picked up the extension at the same time as Jane. Burgess had an easy writing style, kept her interest. She'd never heard of photovoltaic cells, nor did she know anything about photosynthesis or that green plants convert the sun's energy into stored chemical energy. His last paper explained how the sun, a nuclear fusion which already works, is safe 93 million miles away. Solar energy can be stored, that was his theme. She then glanced through a slim volume written by the two men in 1983 which said virtually the same as Paul's earlier papers.

But there was a distinct change in the papers and scripts prepared by Dr Peter Stormont in 1989. His English, for starters, was much more convoluted, but she got the gist. Great strides had been made with photovoltaic cells, which could be utilised to power industry. 'Destroy the nuclear power stations,' he'd written. 'Stop polluting Scandinavia and the North Sea, and use the power of the sun.'

Why had Burgess written nothing since 1983? No time, perhaps, now he'd become a powerful executive. Funny she couldn't think of him as a jetsetter. He'd sounded avuncular over the phone, concerned for the children, but calm, and not too shaken when he heard about Pete's death. A stalwart, unflappable person, a good man to have around in a crisis.

She went to bed early, closed the lined velvet curtains, and browsed through Jane's translation of *The Master Builder*.

A slight crunching noise disturbed her concentration. She listened intently. Bats nesting in the roof? Mice? Rats? She shivered. What did she expect in an old house? There it was again . . . but outside the house . . . footsteps on the gravel path. She was out of bed in a flash, turned off the bedside light, grabbed a torch from her handbag and crept down the stairs. There was a different noise now coming from the kitchen. She stood in the hall until her eyes became acclimatised and then silently eased open the kitchen door. She saw the outline of a tall man outside the back door window. She heard him fiddling with the lock. There was a sudden plop as the inside key fell on the quarry tiles. Silence for a moment, then she heard the lock turn. The man had a key! In a flash she remembered Jane's story about a window cleaner who'd appeared when she was out shopping. Was this the same man? Was he still hoping to find Pete's papers, or plans? If so, he'd get nowhere. She was positive there was nothing to find.

Her first impulse was to turn on the hall light, frighten

the man off, but she controlled her fear. Dare she, had she the nerve to let him carry on? She suddenly realised her car was outside. Why hadn't he noticed it? Then it dawned. Of course, it has to be someone who knows exactly what's going on. Someone who knew she was at Hampton Court, who knew she was with Jane at Lady Stormont's. Someone who presumes I'm still there. There was a glimmer at the top of the stairs thrown by the bedside light. That was a giveaway. Sergeant Mayhew took a deep breath, she'd chance it. There was time to dash upstairs and get dressed. She turned off the light, slipped on a black blouse and jeans, and then with the aid of the torch looked round for something to cover her face. Damn, she'd not even brought a chiffon scarf with her. She'd have to improvise, pull one of her sheer black stockings over her face and trust to providence.

She shook as she stood at the top of the stairs waiting for the man to enter. My God he was cheeky. Came in as though he owned the place, even humming to himself. He knew exactly where he was going, been here before. Straight to the front door . . . pulled down the blind . . . into the study . . . closed the curtains . . . damn, the door had swung to on its own volition. She heard him switch on the anglepoise, and then open a drawer. He took his time, he was careful, painstaking.

Mayhew crept down the stairs; halfway down there was an almighty creak, in the stillness it sounded like thunder. There was no time to move either up or down, all she could do was sit tight and hold her breath. She waited. He pushed the door wide open and stood in the hall listening. She could hear him breathing. Could he hear her? He started humming again, happy now as he returned to his task. Six drawers had been opened and closed. What now? Something was slammed down on the desk. The box files, possibly? Took some time over them. She knew exactly what he was reading, but the

Open Collegiate leaflets and scripts wouldn't help him.

She visualised the desk, could see the telephone and the Cathedral game on the left, and on the right a desk diary, pen holder and selection of pencils. He replaced the box files. What if he'd finished and came up the stairs? Surprise was her only weapon. A karate kick in the groin and a prayer to the Almighty, but he hadn't finished, he too was going through the books. Eventually, it seemed like an eternity, he opened the cupboard under the bookshelves. Hope, she thought gleefully, springs eternal, knowing that *The Mikado*, *Iolanthe* and scores for brass bands wouldn't get him anywhere. He was humming happily again, so what had he found?

Then she panicked, felt sick and mentally kicked herself. Supposing, whatever it was, an invention or outlines for more defence equipment, had been written in code in the Gilbert and Sullivan libretti?

The cupboard door closed. He switched off the angle-poise, opened the curtains and stepped into the hall. His head, on the other side of the bannisters, was so close she could smell his aftershave. He moved quickly to the front door and as he released the blind, one side of the hall was lit by a brilliant shaft of moonlight. He was tall, but his features were in deep shadow on the unlit side of the hall. He walked rapidly into the kitchen carrying something. Dear God, don't let it be the G & S scores. As soon as he'd locked the kitchen door behind him Sergeant Mayhew breathed a sigh of relief. She was sweating so much she needed a bath, but first a double whisky and then a call to Dickybird. Ruin his beauty sleep.

Paul Burgess caught the midnight flight from Malta to Heathrow. Six meetings in two days. The three Maltese and two Italians certainly meant business. The feasibility studies and survey had been completed, but the results hadn't been divulged to the Maltese who were pressing for action. Olio could reap considerable rewards from this latest venture, but they had to be sure, had to make certain that their plans weren't scuppered by recent developments. Two more meetings had been scheduled for the following day, but he'd excused himself, apologised, felt he should be back in England, make sure Jane and the twins were being looked after. They understood. They were all family men. If only Pete had signed the recent proposal drawn up by a caucus of oil producers Jane would now be sitting pretty. £25,000 a year for twenty years, half a million, not to be sneezed at, which together with his pension would have left her comfortably off.

It took some seconds for the bleeping to wake him.

'Yes? Yes?'

'Mayhew here, sir. A recent development, thought you should know.'

'What time is it, for God's sake?'

'Quarter to two. My visitor's just left.'

'And you wake me, Sergeant, to tell me that?'

'An intruder, sir, who had a back-door key. He entered through the kitchen and left the same way.'

'What! Why didn't you call for assistance?'

'No need.'

Struth she's cool. 'So you had a heart to heart, did you?'

'Not quite as close as that, although I could hear him breathing.'

'What was he after?'

'As you said, sir, looking for something in the study. He went through all the drawers, the box files, the books and the cupboard.'

'But you'd been there first?'

'Yes, sir, but . . . but I may have missed something.'

She heard him groan.

'There was a mass of sheet music for brass bands in

the cupboard, and scores for *The Mikado*, and *Iolanthe*. I glanced at the fly leaves, but didn't look further.'

'Nothing loose inside?'

'No, but I wondered whether Pete had used code, either hidden in the musical notation or in the libretti.'

'Are the scores still there?'

'No, sir, they're missing.'

'Damnation!'

'Do you think they held the answer?'

'How the hell should I know? Could have been an avid G & S fan, so now we're looking for a tall man who's a fucking wandering minstrel.'

She was silent.

'Apologies, Sergeant, keep at it, keep looking.'

She put the phone down. Her unconventional boss hadn't got hold of this case. His intuition had let him down.

Byrd knew he'd not get any more sleep. What he really needed was a strong drink, but the cupboard was bare.

Tom Abrams, an early riser, was still feeling angry at Dr Patel's inability to identify the allergy. He'd waited for nearly three hours drinking coffee after coffee, and all he'd got for his pains was a verbal list of toxins which couldn't produce such horrendous swelling. He left the hospital feeling cheated, spent a restless night, and rose the next morning ready to do battle with anyone who stepped out of line.

He'd just popped two pieces of bread into the toaster when the phone rang. Damn they couldn't even let him enjoy his breakfast in peace. 'Abrams,' he said irritably.

'Rangit Patel here, Captain. I've some news for you.'

'You've worked through the night?' asked the astonished man.

'Curiosity, sir, not dedication, that's what drives me on.'

'All right, doctor, let's be having it.'

'The only answer I can come up with is hematoporphyrin. How he took it, when he took it, and where it was manufactured are all questions for the police.'

'You're a wizard, Patel, a bloody wizard. My God!'

'What's the matter?'

'There's a ghastly stink. A chemical change has taken place in the toaster. Bread has turned to charcoal. I'd better deal with it.'

Patel laughed as he replaced the phone.

Byrd rose early knowing a police mechanic would be arriving at six a.m. to repair his own car which had spluttered its way down the Hampton Road, and finally given up the ghost as he drove into the car park in the early hours of the morning. His own fault, he'd disregarded the warning signals on his mad dash up to Bletchingdon to share a late supper with Stephie and Kate. Despite the late meal, and the lack of sleep he could blame on Mayhew, he was dressed and ready for breakfast. If the police mechanic could work miracles he'd nip in to the police canteen in Twickenham.

He was amazed and thankful when he heard footsteps. Ten to six, a bit early for the mechanic, perhaps he too had a lot on his mind and couldn't sleep? When the office door opened the expression of welcome on his face changed to one of disappointment. Breakfast was still a long way off.

'Tom, what are you doing here at this hour?'

'Bringing the good news from Ghent to Aix.'

'Galloped through the night, have you!'

'Patel hasn't been to bed, wouldn't give in, reckons hematoporphyrin is the answer.'

'Hematoporphyrin! Never heard of it. How was it taken?'

'He's not sure, but he's working at it.'

'Good. I'll see him later. Right now I'm going out in search of breakfast.'

'No need, James. Come back with me. I've not eaten yet.'

The Superintendent would have enjoyed his simple breakfast of strawberry muesli, toast and coffee, had the mechanic not told him that his car needed a major operation. It was a dismal start to a day that promised more aggro than the previous eighteen days rolled into one. First Mozart had to be filled in. The latest lab report; the intruder at The Old Rectory; Jane Stormont staying put in the palace; and explicit instructions to his small staff on how to deal with the media. Byrd decided he wouldn't be available for comment.

He arrived at the hospital soon after nine o'clock in the Inspector's car wondering why Wolfgang had been unusually affable. Was he was getting to grips with Charlie and beginning to enjoy the hunt?

Patel, who was working on another recumbent form, yawned. 'Sorry, Super, you're not boring me, just that I need eight hours' sleep.'

'Join the club. Now tell me about the substance that killed Stormont. When was it taken, and was it injected or taken orally?'

'Can't say when it was taken because hematoporphyrin is a compound affected by light. In the dark, porphyrin has no effect, but it is highly reactive to sunlight, even artificial light. Yesterday was a dull wet day, we didn't see the sun until after lunch, but the dose taken by Stormont, which made him extraordinarily photosensitive, would have been lethal in even the most watery sunlight.'

'Could he have taken it the day before?'

'I doubt it. Artificial light in the home would have induced symptoms. Much more likely that it was taken sometime that day.'

'How? An injection?'

'Could have been but there's no trace.'

'In tablet form?'

'Possibly, but the interesting question is how did he get hold of it? It isn't manufactured and sold over the counter.'

'But it could have been prepared with malice aforethought?'

'Yes, Superintendent, you could say that.'

Jane answered the door. For a moment they looked at each other. He noticed her blotched cheeks, the bags under her eyes, the lack of her normal wondrous vitality. She looked at the man she'd known ever since her marriage. Pete's dependable friend, always there in an emergency. He put his arm round her and held her tightly against his chest.

'Come in, Paul,' she whispered. 'The kids will be surprised.'

Lady Stormont, still in bed, recognised his voice, the voice of a man she didn't like who was incredibly generous to her grandchildren, who filled the role of a grandfather. Maybe that's what she didn't like? She decided to stay in bed, having no desire to discuss her son or the manner of his death.

Detective Superintendent Byrd left the hospital in Wolfgang's temperamental ten-year-old car. To begin with it had coughed and groaned but was now happily purring along at fifty. It didn't respond much to pressure, rather like its owner, but that suited the driver. He wanted to think, leisurely driving nearly always produced results. His mind went back to the moment when Kelsoe asked Jane whether Pete was on antihistamine. *No, but he takes Tolbutamide*. That was all, but it was enough. Had someone monkeyed with the prescription? Doubtful, that was taking things a bit far. Then he recalled Mayhew's words in The Little Dog Laughed after band practice. A window cleaner who'd stolen nothing and left the house as he'd found it. No, not quite as he found it, thought Byrd, as he pulled off the road into the next lay-by.

Georgina was in the act of making a shopping list when the phone rang. He didn't waste time with pleasantries.

'Sergeant, nip up to the bathroom, collect all the bottles of pills and medicine you can lay your hands on, and we'll go through them. I'll hold the line. Careful how you handle them, use a towel, we don't want to drive Forensic up the wall.'

'Right.'

She knew by the underlying excitement in his voice that he was on to something. There were two bottles in the bathroom cabinet and three on the windowsill which she wrapped in tissue before dashing down to the study and plonking them on the desk.

'OK, you ready, sir? Rennies, paracetamol, natural vitamin E, Multivite, and a bottle of prescription tablets dated May 30th.'

'That's what we need. How many tablets are there?'

'Difficult to tell, it's half full.'

'Good. Wrap it carefully, get over to Kidlington and leave it with Sergeant Quinney. He'll talk to Forensic.'

'Straight away?'

'Yes, or have you more pressing business?' Damn, why did he always have to rile her?

Jane's just phoned. She'll be here for lunch.'

'What! Didn't she plan spending two days with her mother-in-law?'

'Paul Burgess, the guy who rang from Malta, is driving her home. Can't do it tomorrow, because he has commitments on the island. There's friendship for you, sir.' Now she was getting at him. 'One thing has crossed my mind.' She waited, deliberately.

'Well, come on, share it.'

'I know he's a close friend and all that, but how did a busy man who hops around the universe know where to find Jane on a Sunday afternoon in June?'

'Could have phoned the Old Rectory first.'

'He didn't.'

'You mean there's nothing on the answerphone?'

'No. No message and no one has hung up.'

She heard him give a deep sigh of satisfaction. 'Sergeant, you've earned your keep today.'

As he drove through the Trophy Gate he noticed a tall familiar figure taking pictures. He stopped and hooted.

'What's the matter with you, Lawrence, you're behaving like an American, never seen you with a camera before.'

'All in a good cause, James. I've a commission.'

'You mean you're America's answer to Lord Lichfield?'

'No, I couldn't compete. I doubt if any of these shots will be in focus. They're aide memoires, that's all.'

'For what?'

'I intend to write a book about the influence of the Tudors.'

'I thought the Stuarts were the attraction for both you and your old enemy.'

'What are you getting at?'

'Your latest effort on Monmouth.'

'I was lucky this time. It had good reviews.'

'But not both books, Professor, not the one based on disinformation.'

'"The babbling gossip of the air", James, but if you keep it to yourself I'll give you a signed copy.'

'You can't buy me, Lawrence, but it was a splendid joke, nearly as good as the *Piltdown Man*.'

'It kept me amused.'

'Lawrence, have you a moment?

Something in the policeman's voice caught his interest.

'Plenty of moments, why?'

'Get in the car. I've just had a brainwave. You're the very man.'

They drove in silence, the Professor wondering, the policeman planning. Byrd parked the car in the public car park well away from curious eyes. No one need know about this exercise.

'What's gotten into you, James? Why all the cloak and dagger?'

'Free for the next two or three weeks, are you?'

'Yes.'

'Brenda too?'

'Yep.'

'Care to do a job for me?'

'Not sending me to Switzerland again, are you?'

'No, Malta. How does that dig you?'

'Catacombs, Roman remains, knights whose origins were here in Hampton Court before Wolsey did a takeover, and wondrous churches. Never been there, worth a visit I'd say.'

'Good. Well, this is what I want you to do.'

Byrd smelt the coffee as he walked down the corridor. Things had improved since WPC Shaw had come aboard. Mozart was still tapping away and cursing softly to himself.

'What's the matter, Inspector?'

'I'm a bloody awful typist, and I'm too old to take lessons now.

'But you've made headway.'

'Yes, I've even amazed myself. This is the first time I've ever made a computer work for me. Thought it was a young man's plaything. Incidentally, sir, Miss Moorcroft remembers seeing a man and woman driving out of the car park in a white Cavalier on the day of the murder.'

'Why wasn't this picked up before?'

'Due to my . . .'

'I see. What was odd about it? Why should she remember?'

Because they stopped for a second man who came running. He threw himself into the back seat and they were off.'

It was evident to Byrd that Wolfgang was through the pain barrier as far as computers were concerned, and had discovered another piece of the puzzle which fitted perfectly.

'Now that you're an expert, Inspector, tell Charlie we need everything he can dredge up on Sir Hubert Morrissey's chauffeur.'

Mozart frowned, he wasn't all that expert, was his boss being sarcastic?

'The man on the spot, the fly on the wall?'

'Exactly.'

He'd bloody find out if it was the last thing he did, but first he wanted to know what the Super had turned up.

'Any joy at the hospital, sir?'

'Yes. Another chapter for Charlie to digest.'

Shaw didn't ask. She placed two coffees in front of them while Mozart jotted down the results gleaned from Patel, culminating with the despatch of the pills from the Old Rectory to Kidlington.

'Is that the lot, sir?'

'Yes, for the moment.' Better not mention the Professor's projected trip to Malta.

'Excuse me, sir,' said Shaw quietly, 'Colonel Wishart says the meeting will begin at ten sharp.'

He knew what was coming. It would be worse than the Grand National, too many fences on a dodgy horse.

Wolfgang read the situation, almost felt sorry for him. Another obstacle Dickybird would have to face. He was glad his stint in the Force was nearly over. One more year, and then untold freedom.

'I'll ask a few questions about the chauffeur, record

the autopsy gen, and get everything up to date,' said the Inspector, eager to get back to his toy.

Not quite everything, thought the Superintendent.

Colonel Wishart and Tom Abrams were seated while the bulky figure of Sir Elwyn Rees-Davies effectively blotted out the early morning sun. Heavier by far, and greyer than he was at their meeting in the Tower of London two years ago. Couldn't possibly see the ball any more with that paunch. Sir Elwyn turned to look at the man whose appearance belied his occupation. A dark purple shirt, no tie, and jeans. Could easily be an artist, actor, or jazz musician. Never a policeman. He might get away with it in Oxfordshire, but it wouldn't be accepted in the Met. A mistake, perhaps, to have asked Suckling to second him. Hadn't hit it off with Sir Hubert who was furious at being questioned about his staff. It didn't do to upset the Minister, to cast aspersions about his employees who'd all been vetted. He was even more annoyed about being bugged in the State Apartments, though he could hardly lay the blame at Byrd's door. Morrissey on the previous evening had descended on him, ruined his game of bridge, persisted with the notion that Dr Stormont's death was unnatural, wanted to know the findings of the autopsy as soon as possible. Wanted Byrd off the case. Oddly the Colonel, who was nobody's fool, still had faith in this maverick policeman.

'Sit down, Mr Byrd. I'll not beat about the bush. I'm being pressured by the Minister of Defence to hand over the case to Special Branch or MI5. "National importance" is the Minister's song. I may be forced into an action I don't want to take, but there's no escaping the fact that both the palace and the police are receiving a bad press. Stalemate on Veasey and Jackson, and now the loss of one of our most brilliant scientists. I want to know what's going on, Superintendent. You've seven days to come up with something, and for that respite you have to thank the Colonel.'

A wry smile flickered over Byrd's face as Tom Abrams winked at him.

'Before you give us a résumé,' continued Sir Elwyn, 'I have to tell you that I've increased the strength of the Force here to deal with the influx of visitors, and the media, photographers, TV crews and reporters who think they have the right to go where they like, do what they like.' The Colonel buzzed his secretary. 'We'll have coffee now, Miss Moorcroft.' She knew by the sound of his voice he was having a difficult morning. As if the fire in '86 hadn't created enough endless problems without two murders and the inexplicable death of Dr Stormont whom she'd often seen wandering round the gardens with his mother. He'd always looked as fit as a flea. A terrible way to go, in front of his children, too. There was an uncomfortable silence as she entered.

'Shall I pour, sir?'

'No, leave it to Tom.'

She was glad to get out of the office where the vibes were distinctly unfriendly. Less than a month ago she'd looked forward to her work, never a dull moment, a happy place enlivened by the Colonel's wicked sense of humour, but life had changed. Retirement, after all, might not be such a bad idea. Better than all this aggro.

James Byrd stirred his sugarless coffee thoughtfully. How much should he disclose? There were strands as fine and breakable as a spider's web, ideas . . . maybe not too fantastic . . . feelings which he couldn't ignore, a scenario in which Mayhew and Lawrence played important roles. There was no point in mucking about, a short cut was the answer. Unethical but he'd no choice. If the Commissioner wanted a result in seven days the game had to be played his way, even if he lost his head in the attempt. He could always teach languages, although conjugating verbs was hardly a vocation.

Sir Elwyn took off his glasses to clean them. He huffed on them, puffed on them, polished them, and he put them on again. Even clean they didn't improve the view. The same purple shirt, the same dark hair, the same beard.

'Well, Superintendent, we're waiting.'

'It's coming together, sir, but it's imperative we hold the inquest tomorrow. If the verdict is death through inexplicable natural causes, a change, say, in the metabolism due to the dead man's diabetes, it will give me room to manoeuvre.'

'We can't play around with findings, Byrd, and you know it.'

He went on as though the Commissioner hadn't spoken. 'The pathologist has identified the agent which resulted in death, but he's far from satisfied, because there was hardly any trace of Tolbutamide which Stormont took daily. He feels that another substance, which he's identified as hematoporphyrin, caused a reaction. What he can't say is whether it was self-administered, taken inadvertently or fed to him by other means.'

'Poison, Superintendent, was Sir Hubert's diagnosis without even seeing the event.'

'I'd rather, sir,' he replied quickly, 'that at this stage Sir Hubert is not informed. Let's get the inquest over first.'

'Why?'

'Someone in the Minister's office knew exactly where he'd be on the day that Veasey and Jackson were murdered. That person is crucial to the enquiry, and I want him to believe that the case has reached an impasse.'

'I'm sure, Mr Byrd, that won't be difficult.'

Byrd returned to the Incident Room followed by Tom Abrams. It all depended now on Charlie regurgitating info on the Minister's chauffeur. The Inspector gave him thumbs up when he entered the room and handed over two print-outs. A photograph and details of Raymond Simmons.

SIMMONS Raymond
Born 1956
Present address:
115 Veronica Road, Tooting, SW17
Joined the Coldstream Guards in 1977, aged 18
Married 1980
Transferred to SAS 1982
Attained rank of Sergeant August 1983
Broke back parachuting 1989. Invalided out on full pension.
Recovered but left with permanent weakness.
Taken on as chauffeur by the Ministry of Defence

The photograph told him nothing. A bland face, hardly lined, sensual lips, hair cut short. Legend underneath read, 'Raymond Simmons, aged 35, 5′8½″, mousey hair, hazel eyes, slight limp.'

'SAS, that was your mob, Tom. Did you know a Raymond Simmons?'

'No.'

'Take a look at the photograph and description.'

'Good God, this chap was here on Sunday . . .'

'What!' shouted the two policemen in unison.

'On the back row with a woman. Took the last two seats.'

'Struth, what a break. Now, we need someone to check his movements over the weekend. Lives in Veronica Road, Tooting.'

'Sir,' said a quiet voice in the corner.

The three men turned to look at WPC Shaw.

'My mother lives in Bushnell Road, it's very close . . . I could . . .'

Mozart laughed. 'Here we go again, Miss Marple to the

rescue.'

'You're absolutely right, Inspector,' said Byrd, silencing him with a look.

'Constable, get home, a police car will drop you, change into civvies, visit your mother, find out how Simmons spent his weekend and get back here with the answer before the day's out.'

'Yes, sir,' said Shaw grinning from ear to ear.

She looked down on the coastlines of England and France thinking it was the sight a bird would see on a clear day. The Channel, once England's natural protection, no longer kept an invader at bay, not according to Lawrence who said the French were taking over by more subtle means. Shares in our water, shares in our electricity, buying out electronic and computer firms and exporting vast quantities of food and wine to Albion.

Brenda glanced at her husband who'd no eyes for the view. His head, as usual, was buried in a book. This time, however, several books, all guides to Malta.

In all her twenty years married to Steve he'd never done anything on the spur of the moment. Poor Steve, if he could see her now he'd not believe the change, nor would he believe Lawrence had walked into the cottage at three o'clock and said, 'Pack your bags, we're catching the eight o'clock plane to Malta.'

So far he'd not explained this sudden desire to examine Roman remains. His speciality was Tudor and Stuart England, why had he developed this particular bug? Brenda never asked, she bided her time, she got there in the end.

The plane landed on time, and to her amazement she was left to deal with their scanty baggage while Lawrence dashed to a telephone. That's why he'd asked the air hostess for plenty of small change. Now what was her uncommunicative husband up to?

Professor Lawrence Berkeley had done his research. First he rang Trusthouse Forte in Valletta to ask whether a Mr Paul Burgess was staying there. He drew a blank which didn't surprise him. Finding him could be a long haul. Malta, stiff with hotels, apartments and holiday complexes, was kept alive by its tourist trade. He might even be aboard one of the luxury yachts in the harbour, in which case he'd never find him.

He glanced down the list of hotels; five star first, and then four star.

The Holiday Inn at Sliema came up with a Mr and Mrs Burge on holiday for a fortnight. If James is right, he thought, this is no holiday.

The receptionist at the Hilton took an unconscionable time; he could hear a cacophony of American and German voices. Two parties must have arrived at the same time. Then a quiet voice, 'Sorry to keep you waiting, sir. Mr Burgess has just arrived back, he's in Room 405, shall I put you through?'

'No, not at the moment. Can you fix me up with a double room for three days?'

'Yes, sir. Room 302, with a sea view.'

Eureka! he breathed.

Brenda waited patiently by the carousel until her husband arrived, looking extraordinarily pleased with himself.

'Sorry to dash off, Brenda, but I wanted to get our accommodation sorted. We'll be staying at the Hilton.'

She was staggered. 'Are you feeling OK, Lawrence?' He nodded.

'Well, what are we celebrating? You're not usually so extravagant.'

'One of these days I'll tell you, but for the moment let's enjoy ourselves.'

Brenda couldn't believe her good fortune. She stood on the balcony gazing down on a vast pool and beyond that the sea. The place had everything. In the morning she'd take a sauna and get her hair done. For three days she'd live like a millionairess and enjoy every moment of it.

Lawrence waited until she was in the bath before mentioning he was going to take a look round. He left her in a great foam of contentment.

First of all he had to find out how long Burgess was staying, whether he was alone in the hotel, and where his meetings were held.

He trudged around several bars until he heard a waiter speaking Italian. Talking to the man in his own language might result in a rapport which could be profitable. After Lawrence had downed three dry martinis the man became quite chatty. His wife and children, who he planned to bring over when he'd saved enough, were living in a poverty-stricken area in the south of Italy. Lawrence tipped him lavishly before asking about the guests. Told him he had a worthwhile proposition to discuss, but didn't want to approach Burgess out of the blue in case he was here on business. Luigi had no idea who Burgess was, but he liked the sight of a crisp English £20 note. The Professor was gulping the last drops of his fifth martini when Luigi bustled across in a state of great excitement.

'He's here, sir,' he whispered.

'Where?'

'In the next bar with two men who both live on the island. The Italian runs a hotel, and the other man's a local, owns that large pharmacy near Marks & Spencer'.

'What's his name?'

'Vella, Matthew Vella. He's not short of the ready, has a holiday villa on Gozo, and a large house in St Paul's Bay.'

'Where do they hold their meetings?'

'Not sure, sir, but I'll find out.' He took the banknote, smiled his thanks and went back to the kitchen from whence all secrets emanated.

7

WPC Betty Shaw didn't bother to go home. Why waste time when her mother's clothes fitted her? She persuaded the driver to take her direct to Bushnell Road. Constable Plowright didn't need much persuading, hadn't Shaw the best legs and the liveliest personality on the station?

Her mother was deadheading roses in the front garden when the police car pulled up. For Mrs Shaw, one of the world's great worriers, a police car stopping outside her house presaged disaster. What had happened to Betty? Had she been shot like that poor girl outside Harrods? She ran towards the car waving the secateurs, but was stopped in her tracks as Betty stepped out of the car.

'What's the matter? Are you ill?'

'No, of course I'm not, Mum.'

The driver laughed. 'Mothers, they're all the same.'

'I'm here on a job, Mum, so put the kettle on while I get dressed.'

Mrs Shaw was used to both her daughters ransacking her wardrobe. Mostly it was tights they borrowed but never returned, or scarves and hats. Betty surprised her by coming down in a plain white blouse which she hadn't worn for two years, and a drab brown skirt that had seen better days.

'What are you doing? You can't go out looking like that.'

'I need to look like a market researcher. There wasn't much time to prepare so I grabbed a clipboard and paper which I must doctor.'

Her mother looked on while her daughter, using a fine black felt-tip, made a reasonable job of producing a questionnaire.

'Market research, Betty? Does that mean lots of questions?'

'Yes, Mum, don't ask because I'm not going to tell.'

Mrs Shaw sighed. 'You don't change, do you?'

'It's best you don't know otherwise you'll be chatting to Maggie next door and it'll be all over the street by tea-time.'

'That's mean, Betty, nothing exciting ever happens here.'

'I know, Mum, but there's nothing exciting about this, so why don't we drink our tea before it gets cold.'

Betty took evasive action, deciding not to go direct to Veronica Road in case her mother was watching. Instead she made for Terrapin Road, walked up the hill and then down Veronica thinking it was essential to have a rehearsal. She decided to try out her questions on an unsuspecting householder three or four doors away from the Simmonses. There's no doubt that despite the seedy nature of some of the houses, Veronica Road, a late Victorian eruption, had style, but like many London streets the double-fronted houses had no garages which meant cars were parked in the road nose to tail. Being an interviewer was much harder than she'd imagined. Mrs Holt who answered the door at 109A was old, suspicious and kept her standing on the step. They were the wrong questions for the wrong person but she had to go through with it.

How did Mrs Holt spend her leisure time? Did she have a holiday? What did she do in the evenings, and how did she spend her weekends? Did she make use of the leisure facilities provided by Wandsworth?

Mrs Holt gaped at the stupid woman standing on her doorstep.

'Bloody silly questions for someone of my age, but I suppose it provides the likes of you with a living.'

She then shut the door with a certain amount of venom, leaving the intrepid interviewer biting her lip and swearing under her breath.

Slowly Shaw made her way to 115, a house with a small front garden lovingly cared for, and the exterior recently painted. Even the brass letter box shone like old gold. She was not surprised to find it divided into four flats, but why weren't they numbered 115A, B, C, and D? She pressed the bell alongside the name of Simmons, and within seconds a voice echoed round the porch.

'Who is it?'

'Elizabeth Shaw. I'm carrying out a market research survey on leisure, and have been given your name.'

'Will you keep me long?'

'Fifteen minutes at the most.'

'Ok. Come on up, then. I'm on the first floor.'

She pushed open the front door and found the interior as spotless as the exterior. The patterned Victorian floor tiles were immaculate, could have been laid yesterday. On the left of the hall was a solid Victorian table with four trays marked A, B, C, and D all holding letters for the respective flat. Very neat, she thought. That's why numbers outside are superfluous. The stair carpet was thick and smelt new, not cheap either. A well-built cheerful-looking woman in her late thirties opened a mahogany door on the landing.

'Come in, Miss Shaw, you're lucky to catch me. Another five minutes, I'd be gone.'

'Sorry about that. Would you rather I came back later?'

'Oh no, fifteen minutes is neither here nor there.'

Betty Shaw picked her way round an assortment of boxes, all containing food, which were strewn all over the floor in the small hallway.

'Come into the kitchen, then you can use the table.'

Sally Simmons turned off the dishwasher. 'It's a noisy beast, but I'd not be without it. Now what is it you want to know?'

'First of all are you single or married, and what is your occupation?'

'I'm married, and I suppose you could call me a peripatetic caterer.'

'You dash into other people's houses and do dinners and anniversaries?'

'Yes, you've got the idea.'

'Are you finding enough work during the recession?'

'More, far more. It's a bonanza because it's cheaper for people to entertain lavishly at home instead of dashing up to town for an expensive dinner and on top of that having to drive back. Business has been so good that I've had the house painted and new carpets throughout the flat.'

'Don't you all share the costs?'

'We own the house, and let the other three flats. That way we choose our neighbours.'

Sally Simmons readily answered question after question. Shaw learnt that they always holidayed abroad, that they entertained a lot and went out most weekends.

'What,' asked Shaw softly, 'did you and your husband do last weekend?'

'On Friday night we went round to my mother's. Saturday, my husband was working and I had a dinner to prepare for twelve in Streatham, and on Sunday we spent the afternoon at Hampton Court.'

'You mean Hampton Court Palace?'

'Yes.'

'Sightseeing, were you?'

'No. There was a sort of pageant, all the fun of the fair, a bit classy, madrigals, Punch and Judy, brass bands, that sort of thing.'

'It was good, was it?'

'No, not as good as it should have been because the poor

guy conducting the brass band collapsed. He died later, I gather.'

'So the band gave up?'

'No, they were most courageous. They gave a concert, a little subdued, but the English spirit came through, guts, that's what they had.'

'Thanks, Mrs Simmons, you've been most helpful . . . just one more question and I'll be off. What does your husband do?'

'He's a civil servant . . . works in Whitehall.'

There was a finality Shaw recognised in the way Sally Simmons said Whitehall.

A thoughtful Police Constable strolled back to Bushnell Road. A civil servant in Whitehall was a high-falutin description for a chauffeur. Might interest the Super!

Tom Abrams put his head round the door.

'Have you a moment for a brief stroll, James, before lunch? Something you should see.'

As they crossed Clock Court Abrams noticed his companion gazing up at the Astronomical Clock.

'It was made for Henry VIII in 1540, but they don't make them like that any more. As you can see it has only one hand, shows the hour, the sign of the Zodiac, indicates the phases of the moon and the time of high water at London Bridge, but its greatest talking point, which our tour guides never miss, is in the centre. See how the sun revolves round the earth, designed long before Galileo made his discovery.'

'Fascinating, but you didn't bring me here to show me a clock so where are we going?'

'To the Renaissance Gallery.'

As they passed through several rooms Abrams exchanged pleasantries with the warders, addressing them all by their christian names. He stopped to ask after the sick wife of Bill Owens who looked as if he could do with a night's sleep, which gave Byrd a chance to take a close look at a vast picture depicting a Lord Mayor's Procession on the River Thames. The large gaily painted barges bedecked with hundreds of flags carried as many as twenty oarsmen in the stern, musicians in the prow, and at least forty passengers all in their finery. As the procession passed Whitehall Palace Charles II could be seen on the balcony enjoying the spectacle. Small cannons emitted white clouds of smoke as they fired salutes, and hundreds of small craft joined in the celebration.

'That was the seventeenth century's answer to the M1,' laughed Tom. 'A river from which there was no return, if you happened to fall into it.'

'You mean it was a sewer?'

'Worse than anything we've suffered in the twentieth century. Now, come and take a look at the most peaceful place in the entire palace.'

Byrd followed him into a room no more than fifteen feet square.

'Look at it, James, look at it! Where else in the world would you find four perfect masterpieces, a Titian, Corregio, Raphael and Bellini all in one small room?'

How strange, thought Byrd, that the tough ex-SAS captain knew exactly what he needed. There was peace. Tranquillity in the face of Raphael's young man, repose in the Bellini, it slowed him down. The aggro of the morning faded, and vague indefinable thoughts were forming a pattern. Half an hour later while he was enjoying a snack lunch in Tom's kitchen the phone rang bringing him down to earth. The inquest had been arranged for the following morning in a State Room in St James's Palace. The same room in which the the inquest on Doris Veasey and Sarah Jackson had taken place.

'She was quite open with me, sir. I didn't get the feeling that there was anything . . . anything doubtful going on.'

Byrd half smiled at WPC Shaw. He never dismissed feelings. So often one's initial instinctive reaction was proved right.

'There's only one thing that struck me as odd.'

'Yes?'

'When I asked what her husband did, she said he was a civil servant, in Whitehall.'

'That's correct.'

'But don't you find it a grandiose description for a chauffeur, sir?'

'Maybe, but I've no doubt his wife's learnt to be circumspect. He was in the SAS, she'd have kept her mouth buttoned. So what did he do over the weekend?'

'Saturday he chauffeured Sir Hubert Morrissey; Sunday morning dug his mother's garden, and on Sunday afternoon he and his wife went to Hampton Court.'

'Why should they do that?'

'It has childhood memories, his father used to take him there as a boy. It all checks out, sir.'

'Does it?'

But he wasn't satisfied. Subterfuge to a man with Simmons' background would be child's play.

The Coroner listened carefully to the evidence, saw no reason to suspect foul play. Understood that the dead man was a diabetic, understood that an outside agent, namely hematoporphyrin, created a change in the metabolism causing Dr Stormont to become photosensitive. No evidence was produced to show how the dosage had been administered. Accidental death was duly recorded and the body released. The result gave James Byrd the leeway he needed. Somewhere out there he knew the murderer would be laughing, feeling safe, carefree and hopefully careless.

Lawrence waited until he'd heard Brenda make an

appointment for a facial and hairdo before venturing forth.

Vella's Apothecary was his objective. Adjacent to Marks & Spencer, Luigi had said. The shop was crowded with holidaymakers all eager to be parted from their shekels by buying expensive perfumes, cosmetics and suntan lotions. He was not surprised, exactly what he'd expected. It was no good trying to merge, he was a head taller than most of the shoppers. Instead he stopped, evinced an interest in a couple of posters while trying to spot the man who'd been in the Hilton.

'Should be good,' said a woman next to him. Only then did he read the poster advertising the St George Operatic Company.

'Wonderful society, they do two a year. *Gondoliers* this week, and *Iolanthe* just before Christmas.'

'Must take my wife,' he said looking down on the grey hair of a local resident.

'She'll love it, you can buy tickets here,' said the lady with merry brown eyes, looking up at him. 'Mr Vella's playing that celebrated, cultivated, underrated nobleman, the Duke of Plaza Toro.'

Underrated, he thought to himself.

'Madam, your enthusiasm is catching. I'll take your advice and get tickets for tonight's performance, here and now.'

During the afternoon Lawrence and Brenda caught the fifty-three bus to Mosta, in a vehicle at least thirty years old, with no suspension and stinking of diesel. When they found themselves in the cool of the parish church they decided the ghastly journey had been amply rewarded. In a small town in the centre of the island they discovered one of the largest and most impressive domes in the world. Modern by ecclesiastical standards, built in the nineteenth century and containing several evocative pictures by local artists. The church was blissfully cool, but outside the temperature unbearably hot, so they sat for nearly an hour, Brenda wondering why they were in Malta, and Lawrence thinking about an affluent chemist.

Lady Stormont concentrated on the stone figures of musicians which adorned the capitals. She tried to conjure up the stonemason, who centuries long gone had lovingly carved them, but it was no good, her mind like a continuous disc returned to the same question. *Why Peter? Why*?

Determined not to give way she took a deep breath, did as the child beside her was doing, clenched her fists, looked straight ahead not daring to catch her daughter-in-law's eye.

Jane glanced at the children who sat waiting for the coffin to arrive . . . it should have been her grandchildren sitting beside her . . . fifty years hence . . . not now. She was dreading the get-together afterwards. Colleagues of Peter's she didn't know, Paul and Anthea being over protective, relations she hadn't seen for yonks, villagers, Sir Hubert Morrissey, though why he'd come she couldn't imagine, and Superintendent Byrd. She'd seen him sitting at the back when she entered. He looked different, a dark suit and a dark green tie, with Stephanie sitting beside him hatless. She'd also noticed Georgina sitting at the back in front of the Byrds. What would she have done without her? She'd coped with everything in readiness for the wake. What a blessing fate had intervened. She'd been about to tell Sergeant Georgina Mayhew to get lost when she found she was playing hostess to a police spy, but at that moment Stephen fell off the swing. His cries interrupted an acrimonious discussion causing them to rush out into the garden to give first aid. By the time his knee had been washed and bandaged her spleen had evaporated. Georgina stayed.

* * *

The small church of St Peter's was full for the first time since Easter Sunday, and as the notes of the Bach fugue faded there came a new sound as the band outside the church began playing the Slaves' Chorus from *Nabucco*. They played it for their conductor who'd once, laughingly, told them that it was the only music he wanted at his funeral. Slowly through the south door came the bearers carrying the coffin on their shoulders. They processed more slowly than usual allowing the band time to reach the final chord. Once the coffin was in position beside the pulpit they retreated quietly to join the bandsmen who remained standing at the back of the church.

Byrd had been one of the first mourners to arrive. He may have looked as though he were praying but he mentally documented everyone who entered. Paul and Anthea Burgess had followed the family and sat behind them on the right of the church. After them came a group of six men and two women, the women didn't seem particularly linked to the men. In fact one of them had no rings on at all. They looked like colleagues from Oxford. He was surprised to see Sir Hubert Morrissey. What was a busy Minister of State, who wasn't that close to Stormont, doing here? Was it all part of the plan to ease him off the case, and it it were what could he hope to achieve at a funeral? It could, of course, work both ways. There were questions the Minister could answer . . . there wouldn't be a better opportunity, and if the chauffeur was around Mayhew could get out there and exert her charm. He leant forward, much to the annoyance of Mrs Smithy, and whispered in the Sergeant's ear. She gave an imperceptible nod before turning her full attention on the speaker.

Paul Burgess stood in front of the lectern delivering an encomium on his past student and friend. He told the story of the gradual change in their relationship, quietly and humbly, how slowly and surely the pupil had become the master, and how proud he was of his ex-student and how grateful.

'Peter's work,' he said, 'would never have been finished, he had the mind and imagination of a Leornardo. Sadly for us all he died at the age of thirty-eight a great loss to the country which has benefited from his genius and imagination, and a loss deeply felt by his friends here today. Our hearts go out to Jane, Sandra and Stephen and Lady Stormont.'

There was more, but he found it impossible. He returned to his seat, closed his eyes and bowed his head.

Jane didn't cry, she felt this was happening to someone else. At any moment the picture would dissolve and she'd find things as they were, the nightmare over. Lady Stormont felt choked, but she sat immobile making no move to mop up the tears.

During the final hymn Sergeant Mayhew and the Superintendent slipped quietly away. It was a blessed relief to escape from the church where the air was charged with love, sadness and anger. Anger that a young man who'd been at the centre of village life should be untimely snatched from their midst.

'You do what you have to do, Sergeant, and I'll bide my time.'

The hearse, parked in front of The Little Dog Laughed, glistened in the late morning sun. There'd be no journey to the crematorium, because Jane loathed the idea, but she had followed her grandparents' wishes to the letter and scattered their ashes on the waters of Lake Windermere. Peter had left no such instructions. He would be given a proper burial in hallowed ground on the west side of the church. No headstone to adorn the grave but a slender marble cross, eight foot high, which she could see from her bedroom would be a constant reminder of the only man she'd ever wanted, trusted and loved.

Mayhew made her way to the Rolls which was parked

behind the hearse. Simmons was sitting there, his hat off, and the windows open listening to pop music. As she made her way down the path towards the lychgate she was stopped in her tracks by the sound of the 'Last Post', which sent shivers down her spine.

Simmons and his pop music annoyed her. She knew she was being unreasonable, but there he sat, enjoying life while Jane and her family suffered, and if Byrd's hypothesis was right he was the one person who knew exactly when and where Sir Hubert met Peter Stormont.

Simmons watched her as she crossed the road, wondering why she'd left the church in such a hurry. There was something about the way she moved. He'd seen it so often when men had been given orders to attack. He wasn't in the least surprised when she spoke to him.

'You are Sir Hubert's chauffeur, aren't you?'

'Yes.'

He turned off the radio and stepped out of the car. 'What's the matter?'

'Nothing. We just thought you might be getting stewed in the car . . . it's a hot day . . . we wondered whether you'd care for a cool drink, in the house, of course?'

'No, ma'am, I can't do that. I never leave this baby. Besides, I have ice-cool drinks aboard.' He gave her a quizzical look, both open and questioning. 'It's a kind thought, but the Minister won't be staying.'

She gave nothing away.

'He's on his way to GCE in Coventry, thought he'd kill two birds with . . .'

He stopped suddenly. 'Sorry about that . . .'

The slightest of smiles flickered across her face. 'That's OK. I'll get back.'

'You were there,' he said softly, 'when it happened?'

'Yes. How'd you know?'

'Saw you. My wife and I were there to enjoy the fun, but it wasn't fun.'

'What made you go to Hampton Court?'

'Nostalgia, I suppose. My dad used to take me there practically every weekend when I was a child.'

She nodded.

He was right, that's what she wanted to know.

Sir Hubert let the last note of the salute die away before making a quick move towards the south door. Len Smithy sniffed his disapproval. Coffin first, and then family. Didn't these people know the drill? First the artist, who he thought had taste, then the policeman, and now another ignoramus he'd never seen before. Why couldn't they wait five minutes? The Minister walked swiftly down the path between the yews towards the lychgate where he found his way barred.

'I'm in a hurry, Mr Byrd.'

'Five minutes, sir. Could fill in a lot of gaps.'

This infuriating man, Morrissey realised, wasn't asking, he was ordering.

'I've an important meeting in Coventry at one o'clock.'

Lunch, thought Byrd, which can wait.

'Murder is important, Sir Hubert.'

'Of course it is,' he growled.

'And this is no ordinary murder.'

'No murder, Mr Byrd, can be described as ordinary.'

'I have a strong feeling, sir, that you may be able to give me a lead.'

The Minister pursed his lips. Almost under his breath, 'Why should I be able to do that?'

'You were worried enough to contact the Commissioner immediately you heard that Stormont had died.'

'That's because I knew him . . . because I . . .'

Sir Hubert knew that one day he'd have to face the issue squarely. He'd always hoped it would go away, solve itself, but it was too big . . . too involved.

'Why were you so keen, sir, for MI5 or Special Branch

to take over the case? Is there something you want hushed up? Something that will rock your government?'

They could hear the low hum of voices as the congregation left the church.

'We'd better talk in the car,' said Morrissey glancing towards the Rolls, surprised to see Simmons standing in the road chatting up a woman.

'Better out here, sir.'

'Damn you, you still suspect my staff.'

'I have to suspect everyone.'

'Well, get on with it, man. What do you want to know?'

'Two things. First of all was Simmons fully employed last Saturday?'

'Yes,' snapped the Minister. 'All day. From eight in the morning until nearly midnight. I was in Manchester. And what else d'you want to know?'

'Exactly what Stormont was working on before the Defence contract came up?'

The policeman looked the Minister straight in the eye. Sir Hubert didn't flinch. He was an inherently honest man, but like all politicians could recycle the facts to suit his case. He sat down under the porch of the lychgate considering all the implications while villagers, who were too many for Jane to cope with in the Old Rectory, streamed down the path, across the road, and into the pub where Luigi, who thought a binge-up unseemly, had coffee and biscuits ready for them.

Byrd saw Georgina shake hands with Simmons and return to the Old Rectory without glancing in his direction.

The Minister took his time, waited for the last person to leave the church, noticed Simmons was back in the driving seat, and wondered how much his willing servant had overheard during the past few months.

'Yes,' he said at last. 'I knew what Stormont was doing, but hardly a motive for murder, and yet . . .'

The policeman sat down facing him, saying nothing.

'You see, Mr Byrd, I don't like admitting, even to myself, the horrendous possibilities. Graft in high places, unscrupulous financiers, respectable international companies, even members of the Government involved in a shameful conspiracy. I have no proof, and I hope to God I'm wrong.'

'You're not wrong, are you, sir? You're spot on.'

For ten minutes the Superintendent sat and listened to the most informative and enlightening exposition since the opening of the case.

He waited until the Silver Rolls had glided out of the village before making tracks for his own car which thanks to the mechanic's ministrations was going like a bird.

Mozart answered his call.

'What have you got for me, Inspector?'

'Some fine dabs on the bottles which Sergeant Quinney took to Forensic, and some foreign bodies in the bottles.'

Mozart didn't hurry. He enjoyed imparting information slowly, especially to Dickybird who, he knew, would be clutching the receiver with hot sticky paws.

'Come on, man, what gives?'

'Four tablets, slightly larger than the Tolbutamide pills, containing enough hematoporphyrin to kill a heavyweight boxer.'

Byrd breathed out slowly. 'Can the dabs be matched?'

'No, sir. No chance.'

But I've a chance, right now, thought Byrd.

'Thanks, Inspector. Expect me first thing in the morning, and arrange a meeting for ten o'clock. I want everyone there, including Captain Abrams.'

'One thing more, sir. There was a call from that Professor chap. Wants you to ring him back.'

'Ring him, where?'

'In Malta, sir, said you'd know where.'

Mozart replaced the phone. His boss wasn't the only one with intuition. Cypriots my foot, they were Maltese. He ran a check on the computer. Yes, it tied up very nicely with Burgess, that oil tycoon who rang from Malta on the day Stormont died.

Lawrence, suffering from too much sun, was sitting on his bed reading when the phone rang.

'Anything to report, Lawrence?

'Gleanings of a quiet ear.'

'Go on. I'm listening.'

'I've checked out all the men our protagonist has met including the leading geophysicist from Olio. Discussions at their last meeting here in the Hilton were decidedly acrimonious.'

'How do you know?'

'I had someone inside.'

'You what!'

'They drink a lot in this climate, which gave an impecunious waiter, who shall be nameless, an opportunity to be in and out of the room. Mostly in, I'm glad to say. Olio has been carrying out a survey on an outcrop of sedimentary rock on the seabed in the vicinity of a small island south of Gozo.'

'You mean they expect to strike oil?'

'Quite likely because for years fishermen have been reporting seepages on this charted but unnamed island, which suggests there are large reserves of oil and gas, similar to those found off the coast of Libya. The Maltese, of course, are hoping for a bonanza on a par with the vast reservoir of natural gas discovered at Groningen by the Dutch in '59 which turned their economy round. Edward Gunn, Olio's geophysicist, didn't enthuse about the findings. Said it was early days, said he wanted more time.'

'Don't they need large platforms, a rig and all the gear?

'Not nowadays. Geophysical techniques can probe into the strata beneath without the expense of drilling a borehole.

'The Board of Olio, it seems, is cool about a project in which they'd be partners, but maybe that's a ploy. There's no doubt that a vast field of oil would solve all their economic problems which a chemist, one of the most influential men on the island, pointed out. In fact we met him last night.'

'Engineered, Lawrence?'

'Of course. We saw a performance of the *Gondoliers*, the first Savoy opera I've ever seen. Not quite my scene but Brenda enjoyed herself. The chemist who played Plaza Toro has a superb voice, so we joined the mutual admiration society in the bar afterwards and told him so. It paid off, because on the last night we went to a party at his place in St Paul's Bay.'

'A good party, was it?' asked Byrd thinking about the missing G & S scores.

'Splendid, champagne flowing, caviare par excellence, and the amusing and often bizarre sight of guests shedding their clothes and inhibitions and leaping into the sea. Not our host, thought. He was expounding on the need for Malta to become more aware of its heritage, to fight to preserve its way of life, to keep government firmly in the hands of its own people.'

'You say he's a chemist?'

'Yes.'

'And is his name Vella?'

'Christ, James, how did you guess?'

'Instinct.'

Lawrence laughed. 'A policeman needs a little luck occasionally. Is Vella, Matthew Vella, your man?'

'Yes. Get a photograph if you can.'

'No problem. We have a programme. Photo and bio all for one Maltese pound! I'll fax it.'

'Ta. You can come home now, Lawrence.'
'We're in no hurry, James.'

As Byrd eased his way through the hall of the Old Rectory he saw Georgina handing out sherries as the mourners crowded into the four ground-floor rooms. The children, he'd noticed, were on the lawn playing with their dragon cars, a game Peter had always supervised.

Paul Burgess had made himself comfortable in the study while Anthea dispensed vol-au-vents and sausage rolls in the sitting-room. Stephanie was carrying out a similar duty in the morning-room, and Mrs Smithy was busying herself in the kitchen. Len, the sole representative of the band, was closeted in a corner with Lady Stormont who didn't seem to be listening to a word he was saying.

The Superintendent took a glass in one hand and a sandwich in the other before insinuating himself into the business group from Oxford who were reducing the sherry stocks at an alarming rate.

'You'll miss Pete,' he said to one of the women whose eyes were bloodshot.

'Yes, it will never be the same again.'

'Not for you, Maureen, it won't,' muttered the other woman under her breath.

'You worked closely with him, did you?' asked Byrd quietly.

'Yes, I was his secretary.'

'Must have been a terrible shock, totally disrupting your work?'

She nodded.

'Who's now in charge of development?'

'Moulay here,' said the bitchy woman whose glasses were too large for her tortoiselike face. 'Dead men's shoes and all that!'

'Cut it out, Maggie, remember where you are,' said Maureen bitterly as she made for the door.

'Another deluge of tears, I suppose, in the upstairs loo!'

'Shut up, Maggie,' said Moulay sharply.

She was wrong. Maureen didn't go upstairs, neither were there any more tears. She found a bench in the garden where she sat, an inscrutable expression on her face, watching the children play with their cars.

'Will you enjoy the challenge, Mr Moulay?' asked Byrd softly.

'Vella, my name's Moulay Vella.'

'From Cyprus, are you?' asked Byrd judging that Vella had imbibed sufficient sherry not to jib at being questioned.

'Good God, no. From Malta, the jewel of the Med.'

'That's not what you usually say.'

Vella laughed. 'Well, Maggie, what do I usually say?'

'That it's desperate for finance, the roads need repair, the transport is archaic, imports too heavy, exports too light, the harbour facilities underused, and above all as a nationalist of the first water you want Libya out.'

'What a speech, Maggie, you must listen occasionally!'

'I know very little about Malta,' said the man who was neither interested in his sandwich nor his drink. For a few seconds in the midst of all the chatter a policeman closed his eyes not daring to let the man facing him read his mind. He no longer heard the conversation, he was isolated letting all the pieces fall into place. Matthew and Moulay Vella . . . cousins . . . brothers . . . or father and son? He opened his eyes.

'Is Malta suffering?'

'Not for much longer.'

'Why's that?'

'Despite what Maggie says we're gradually getting the trade balance together.'

'Never been the same since the British left,' sneered Maggie.

'You're wrong again, the British haven't left. There are hundreds living on the island who prefer life in the sun. Now if you'll excuse me I'll have a word with Mrs Stormont.'

Too much of a coincidence, thought the policeman as he watched Vella place his empty glass on a side table before leaving the room.

Now the pieces were beginning to come together. He emptied his glass, swapped it for Vella's which he picked up by the base, and went in search of Mayhew who was busy in the kitchen helping Mrs Smithy with the coffees. 'Hallo, James,' she said playing her part, as though she'd known him all her life. 'You look like the establishment in a collar and tie.'

He scowled at her. 'Where's Jane?'

'In the morning-room.'

Mrs Smithy showed no inclination to carry the coffees anywhere. Len had told her that this policeman was investigating Pete's death, so she was determined not to miss out.

'Georgina,' said Byrd abruptly, as he made a beeline for the kitchen roll, 'you must meet Moulay Vella, he's quite an interesting character.'

Mrs Smithy looked daggers at him, and wondered why he was wrapping a wine glass in paper.

'She'll not have time to say hallo to anyone while this bean feast's going on, and that glass would be better washed properly.'

'I'll find him, James,' winked Georgina, as she picked up a plate of smoked salmon sandwiches, 'while you give Mrs Smithy a hand with the coffee.'

'Hope he likes fish,' murmured Byrd, as he slipped the glass into his pocket before coping with the tray of coffees.

Jane wasn't in the least surprised when he walked into the morning-room with the coffees.

'Playing butler, are you?'

'For a moment or two. Have you seen Moulay Vella?' There was an urgency in his voice. In a flash she understood.

'The study, I think. Here, let me take the tray while you look.'

Georgina's voice clear as a bell came from the study where he could hear her pressing Vella to sample the smoked salmon sandwiches. He noticed as he entered the room that Burgess's sherry and mini sausage rolls were untouched. What had he been doing?

Aware that Byrd was watching him closely Burgess fiddled with a sketch pad left on top of the Cathedral game.

'This yours?' he asked Mayhew.

'Yes.'

'Mind if I take a look?'

'Feel free.'

Moulay sat on the window seat eyeing Georgina up and down, liking what he saw, and losing no time in sussing out that she was single and lived in Kidlington. Once he'd got the picture there was no need to say another word. A silent assignation was agreed. His eyes invited her. She accepted. Satisfied, Byrd sat down on a stool alongside the desk watching Pete's closest friend leaf through rough charcoal sketches of the Old Rectory. The man was uneasy, sweating slightly.

'Good God!' said Vella suddenly as he gazed at the children playing on the lawn.

Georgina looked, saw nothing unusual. A young woman sitting on a bench in the shade and the twins playing with their red and yellow cars.

'Come and take a look at this, Paul,' said Vella, his excitement mounting. In that second Byrd knew. Knew why the dragon cars had been kept in the study. Knew why Peter had supervised the kids' games.

Burgess and Vella rushed into the garden pursued by

Mayhew. Byrd was faster than all three. He picked up Burgess's glass, emptied it into the begonias, ran into the morning room, grabbed Jane and thrust her into the hall and the glass into his pocket.

'Quickly, come with me into the garden. Don't let Burgess or Vella get their hands on the toy cars. It's important.'

They tore outside to find the two scientists staring, incredulously, at cars which needed neither winding nor the aid of electrical impulses to get them moving. The cars raced each other across a large expanse of lawn as if by magic.

'It's the sun,' Jane whispered to Byrd.

'I know.'

From her position in the shade Maureen was able to read every expression on the faces of the two scientists. Fascination, greed, excitement, wonder, satisfaction, a wry smile from Burgess, perhaps, at his own stupidity for taking so long to track down the experiment. What should she do? She'd felt from the start that Pete's death had somehow been connected with this invention. She'd known about the cars for two years, had stayed on after hours typing formula after formula, always destroying evidence and giving Dr Stormont the only copy. There was nothing she could do now, the hounds of hell were at the gates, but she'd reckoned without Jane and her friend Georgina.

'It's time you two came in and had something to eat.'

'We're not hungry, Mummy, let's go on playing.'

'No, Sandra,' said Jane firmly. 'Later, perhaps.'

Georgina picked up the yellow car and took Stephen by the hand.

'Come on, you too, young man.'

'I'm thirsty, it's ever so hot, that's what makes the cars work.'

'Is it?'

'Yes. Dad said to keep them in the sun for two hours before playing the game.'

'What game?'

'The racing game. Mansell against Senna. That's why my car is yellow and Sandra's is red.'

'Let me take a look, Jane,' said Paul holding out his hand for the red car.

'No, not now,' she said sharply, 'you'll only encourage them. They've had enough sun for one day.'

Maureen smiled to herself as their faces changed. Chagrin, disappointment, anger, disbelief and exasperation at being foiled. She almost laughed out loud, managed somehow to control herself, but she was too late. Vella caught the smug smile of satisfaction which lit her face . . . so too did Byrd.

Mayhew, who was in the throes of great excitement, dragged Stephen into the house. She'd surprise the Super, tell him she knew the identity of the intruder, recognised him by his smell, by the sickening waft of aftershave which hit her as he brushed past in his eagerness to get into the garden. She saw herself sitting immobile on the stairs, hearing the intruder breathe, and smelling the same overpowering aroma. He was the right height, the right build, and without doubt the same man who'd done a bunk with the G & S scores.

Byrd kept the two men talking outside while the women shepherded the twins into the kitchen. Jane made them sponge their hands before sending them into the drawing-room to find Grandma.

Mayhew waited until the kitchen was clear before putting the cars in the oven.

'They'll be safe enough there for the time being.'

'Georgina,' whispered Jane, 'that's what this is all about, isn't it?'

'Possibly.'

'Pete was working on a solar car, the dragon cars are the working models.' Her voice shook. 'I can't keep them here.'

'As soon as your guests have gone I'll put them in the Super's car.'

'Put what in my car?' asked Byrd as he walked in the kitchen.

'The dragon cars.'

'No, that's not the answer. I'll take one, but we'll leave the other in the study.'

'Why?' asked the women simultaneously.

'They're prototypes. Targets for industrial espionage. We'll leave one in the study as bait.' Suddenly he had an idea. 'Do your two kids have cameras, Jane?'

'Yes.'

'I need some photographs . . . too obvious if we do it.'

'They're quite good at it, much better than Mother.'

'Suggest to them, will you, that they sit in the garden and snap guests as they leave, not local people, all those who travelled by car.'

'Have they enough film?' asked Georgina.

'Not sure, I'll nip upstairs and check.'

'Could you also suggest . . .' He stopped abruptly as Maureen Kennedy walked into the kitchen.

'I've come to say goodbye, Jane.'

'Not waiting for the others?'

'No.'

'You'll have to watch yourself,' said Byrd.

She was startled. 'Why do you mean?'

'You know all about this toy, don't you?' he said as he picked up the red one.

She nodded.

'You were careless, gave yourself away.'

'Vella's a pig.'

'Why do you say that?'

'Don't know why Pete kept him on.'

'What was his job?'

'Originally he worked with Pete on the development of a cheaply produced solar car capable of competing in the open market with middle range cars, but Vella slowed up the process.'

'How?'

'Kept coming up with the wrong data, or the computer caught a cold and spewed out erroneous info. He also failed to check out recent research on photovoltaic cells, in fact, you could say he was doing a go-slow. In desperation Pete took him off the project and gave him another job.'

'Why didn't he sack him?'

'Better isn't it to have someone you suspect under your nose?'

'How much did he know?'

'Enough, but he's a strange man, he seemed interested, and disinterested. How do you explain that?'

Easily, thought Byrd.

'Has Burgess any interest in the solar car?' asked Mayhew.

'I'm not sure. They were always so friendly . . . it was quite a joke in the office, fly away Peter, fly away Paul, always together, you see, until recently when I heard them having one hell of a row about some sort of payment.'

'When?'

'Six months ago, seven months, not sure.'

'Payment for what?'

'Don't know. Couldn't have been an invention. It was some sort of contract. I think Paul Burgess was offering him £25,000 a year for twenty years.'

'Half a million,' said Jane slowly. 'Why on earth didn't he take it? Now . . . now . . . we'll never know.'

'Oh yes,' said Byrd. 'We will.'

Maureen embraced Jane and kissed her on both cheeks.

'Let me know, Jane, when you're ready for visitors and I'll come straight over.'

'One more thing before you go,' said the Superintendent.

She stopped in the doorway.

'Are there any papers around?'

'What sort of papers?'

'You know what I mean. Plans? Diagrams?'

'There should be. I typed one copy of the final formula which Pete took with him to lodge at the bank. And there's that other document . . . the one Burgess tried to get him to sign . . . I saw him put it in his briefcase.'

'Keys, Miss Kennedy. How many sets were there to Peter's office?'

'Three. Pete had two sets and I had the other.'

'What about the caretaker?'

'He had one key which opened the dividing door between our two offices, in case of fire, but he'd never let that out of his possession.'

She's sharp, thought the Superintendent. 'Thanks, Miss Kennedy, you've been a mine of information.'

She left knowing he would search Pete's office, hers too. She'd no time to destroy the notebook.

'Jane,' asked Byrd softly, 'can you put your hands on Pete's keys?'

'Only the set with his car keys on, the others are missing.'

'Missing!'

'They'll turn up. They always do. He was hopeless, lost them every other day.'

Stephanie appeared at the door. 'Jane, I think you're needed, people are beginning to make a move, most of them going home, but the office crowd is going over to Luigi's.'

'Now, Sergeant,' said Byrd, as soon as the masses had

been despatched and they had the kitchen to themselves. 'What bugs you?'

'I know, sir. I know who broke in that night.'

Byrd gave her a wicked grin. 'Would he hail from a Mediterranean island? Black hair, lean, six foot, a man who's unwittingly dating a policewoman?'

She was furious. 'Why didn't you tell me, sir?'

'I didn't know, not until I spoke to Lawrence Berkeley in Malta after the service.'

'Malta,' she echoed.

'Yes, we'll go into that in the morning. I've called a meeting for ten o'clock, everyone.'

'But what about Jane? She needs me.'

'She's safe enough now. Lady Stormont has agreed to stay on for a couple of days. The Burgesses leave in the morning, no doubt taking a dragon car with them.'

He knew what she was thinking, but she was a policewoman, and if she wanted to become an Inspector she'd better get her priorities right.

'I doubt if there's anything else to find, not here anyway.'

He saw her nostrils dilate slightly, showing exactly what she thought of his methods and his theories.

'Tonight I want you to keep Vella occupied. Dinner at the pub over the road or anywhere that takes your fancy, but not Oxford. Find out what makes him tick.'

'Georgina, Georgina are you ready?' shrieked Sandra, as she ran into the kitchen.

'Ready! Ready for what?'

'You promised to play the Cathedral game.'

'Aren't you tired of it?'

'No. You promised . . .'

'All right. One game only.'

'Do you want to play, Mr Byrd?'

'It's quicker with four,' said Mayhew softly.

'Ok, but as Georgina says, one game and then I'm off.'

It was relaxing, but while he was cogitating on the *modus operandi* for the following morning he got lost amid the Pennines travelling from Durham to Chester. The twins squealed with delight, and proceeded to stymie Georgina's next move to Exeter. She was in two minds, and unconsciously rubbed her fingers up and down the side of the board while she planned her next move. She was about to take a card of Chance from the pack in the middle when she noticed the edge of the thick paper on which the game was printed had come away from the board.

'Half a moment, folks, I'd better fix this.' She licked her fingers, slid them along the underside, and as she did so felt the edges of a paper lodged beneath the surface of the game.

'For heaven's sake, Georgina, stop fidgeting. Let's get on with it.'

'Quickly,' she said, 'remove your counters and the Chance cards.'

It was an order which even her superior obeyed. The astonished players looked on as Sergeant Mayhew slowly and with infinite care extracted a document.

'Nothing here, did you say, sir?' She couldn't resist the jibe.

'My God,' he gasped, 'right under our noses.'

Before she'd a chance to read a word he took it from her hand, gave it a cursory glance, folded it, and put it in his pocket. Morrissey's foul imaginings were spot on.

They heard Paul Burgess speaking to Jane as he came downstairs.

'Quickly,' he said, 'put your counters back. We'll finish the game and repair the board afterwards.' He leant forward, 'Can you children keep a secret, a very special secret?'

'Yes,' they whispered.

'That piece of paper will lead me to the treasure.'

'You mean like *Treasure Island*?' asked Sandra.

'Why can't we see it?' said Steve fretfully.

'It has to be solved by one person and when I've found the treasure I'll send you your share.'

'Promise not to tell,' said Georgina as she put her hand flat on the table and placed their right hands on hers.

'Promise,' they whispered as Burgess walked in.

'My, it's quiet in here. Who's winning?'

'Shush,' said Byrd, 'Georgina's concentrating.'

The twins giggled, but kept their eyes firmly fixed on the board.

8

James Byrd drove Stephanie back to Bletchingdon. He had a quick cup of tea and not having eaten during the wake he put away three poached eggs on toast and half a Genoa cake before changing into black jeans and a black shirt.

'Good God,' said Stephanie as he came downstairs, 'why've you changed your image?'

'To see and not be seen.'

'I see,' but she didn't.

He went straight to Kidlington where Sergeant Quinney, who'd been forewarned, was waiting for two glasses wrapped in plastic bags, a recently discovered document that promised so much for so little and four photographs.

'Get them blown up, Sergeant, fax one to Inspector Mozart and one to Dr Jackson in the States. I want the results of the dabs first thing in the morning. We'll find they match those on the medicine bottle and the shoe.'

'Match, sir, aren't you jumping the gun?'

'Do it, Sergeant.'

'Right, sir,' grinned Quinney, who'd missed his boss despite the fact he always gave him a hard time, but life was never dull with Dickybird around.

Mayhew, disregarding her Chief's instructions, decided to stay another night at the Old Rectory knowing she could reach the palace in time for the ten o'clock meeting.

Moulay Vella wouldn't expect to be invited back to the Old Rectory. She could lead him on without being expected to share his bed. Being forced to have dinner in the line of duty was enough.

There was only one man who occasionally turned her on, but she kept her head, never betrayed an interest; well, almost never. There'd been a fleeting second, no more, when she was working on the Tower case. A look, a feeling, an understanding between them, ephemeral, but she'd never forget. Since her divorce, a blessed release from an ambitious self-centred bank manager, she'd enjoyed her single state, and most of all her single bed. She'd choose, would never be chosen. Not again.

Moulay Vella stayed on at The Little Dog Laughed long after his colleagues had left, confident that Georgina would appear. He was stunned when she sauntered into the pub, a metamorphosis he'd not been expecting. At the funeral she'd looked attractive in a plain blue dress, wearing very little make-up. With a skin and eyes like hers she didn't need cosmetic aids, but here in the bar he saw a totally different personality. A woman heavily made up, tremendous panache, and something else he couldn't quite fathom. There was determination, intelligence, missionary zeal and another indefinable quality. He smiled at his own thoughts. Even missionaries might be good in bed, provided they read the right gospel. The tightly fitting calf-length red dress left little to the imagination. Her make-up defined each feature more clearly and her luscious dark hair had been brushed until it framed her face. She smiled at Moulay as he stood up to offer her a chair.

'You're beautiful,' he said simply.

After great debate they decided to distance themselves from Hanwell-on-the-Hill, a sad sad place, and eat at the Avon, a comfortable restaurant in Avon Dassett four miles away.

She insisted on buying the wine, he didn't demur, he'd

met these independent English women before, liked to break down their defences, adding spice to the encounter.

He was more entertaining than she'd imagined, even fascinating when he forgot about his macho image and talked about Malta.

'You know something, Moulay, I shall spend my next holiday on the island. I must see the glass factories, churches and Roman remains, but why on earth did you leave?'

It was the right question. He gave her a run-down on the economic plight of the island, the lack of jobs, and why as a scientist there was no scope for him on the island.

'Have you a family there?'

'Yes, my parents who live on Gozo, a sister married to an Italian hotelier living on the island, and a brother.'

'What does he do?'

'He's a bright boy, a bio-chemist who could have chosen all sorts of lucrative careers, but he chose to stay. He has four pharmacies which provide a comfortable living, but maybe he'll strike lucky, make a fortune in Malta, so he could be in the right place at the right time.'

What, she wondered, did he mean by that?

'What are his other interests?'

'Tennis, sailing, and singing in the local G & S Society.'

Georgina remembered the figure in the half light walking out of the study carrying something which she later discovered were scores of *Iolanthe*, and the *Mikado*. Thank the Lord, she thought. All he'd done was nick a present for his brother, and not Pete's latest plans.

'Why,' she asked, as a thought flashed through her mind, 'do you think your brother is in the right place? Has he struck gold?'

'Better than that . . . much better . . . I'll tell you one day.'

The way he said 'one day' held promises she'd rather ignore.

* * *

Byrd whistled as he drove to the lab in Oxford with Pete's keys in his pocket, the set with the car key attached. The others were missing. Easy to guess who had them now. Evidence, that's what he needed, concrete evidence. Sir Elwyn, despite his Celtic forbears, wouldn't accept intuition, gut feelings, conjecture, nor a hypothesis that pointed to two men. 'Unwise,' he'd said, 'to have Vella in for questioning until we can charge him with a proven offence. Guesswork's no good. Proof positive, nothing else will do.' Sir Elwyn's maxim made good sense, but there'd be a way to spike the bastard.

He parked the car in the centre of the road between the Sheldonian and Blackwells, before walking back the way he'd come passing Wadham on his right.

There was no one around as he let himself into the Francis Bacon Laboratory. Jane, despite having been in the building only twice had genned him up on the security system. After he'd unlocked the door he had thirty seconds in which to locate a small box hidden behind the porter's desk, and deactivate the alarm. It was enough. The lifts, he knew, were disconnected at night which meant a long climb up to the fourth floor. 'Along the corridor to the left,' she'd said, 'and the last room on the right.' As he walked to the end he read the legend on each door recognising only two, those of Maureen Kennedy, whose room, as he expected, was adjacent to Peter's, and Vella's.

Peter's office was smaller than he'd imagined, full of filing cabinets and diagrams covering every available bit of wall space. The job would take him most of the night, and only thin sun blinds to keep the sunlight out, or artificial light in. He closed them, used the angle poise hoping no one would show any interest in a slight glow on the fourth floor.

Each cabinet was clearly marked, so too were the files.

Maureen had done a good job. The files in the top drawer of the first cabinet were totally devoted to the Open Collegiate studies in photosynthesis. Most of them written by Peter, a few jointly with Paul Burgess and two by Moulay Vella. After four hours Byrd had drawn a complete blank; not only that, but he was tired and cursed himself for forgetting to ring Stephanie to let her know what time he'd be back. Damn . . . damn . . .

Next he tackled Maureen's office. The filing cabinet, securely locked, resisted all his efforts, so he settled himself at her desk and methodically sifted through the drawers. At the bottom of the right-hand drawer he found a blue notebook containing longhand notes which, if he'd been in her place, he would have locked in the impregnable cabinet. Careless girl. Halfway through she'd attempted to write a few lines of verse.

> Dear heart, dear unassuming man,
> How do I hide this love of mine?
> How can I bear to be so close
> Never to touch your hand?
> Nor feel your kiss so light
> Never to be beside you
> In the dark reaches of the night.

He closed the notebook he should never have opened.

Suddenly he had an urge to take a look at Vella's office. Surprisingly it wasn't locked.

The filing had no system, neither alphabetical nor chronological. It would take him hours, which he hadn't got, to do a thorough search. Disappointed and frustrated he sat down at the desk and went through the drawers. Four were jammed with scientific journals and unanswered letters, but in the fifth he struck gold. At the bottom of the drawer underneath a load of articles on photosynthesis he discovered a paper which could convict a man, and had precipitated another's death. He shouted, as one man in his bath had shouted many centuries before, 'Eureka!'

Sergeant Mayhew, who'd expected a traffic-free journey down the M40, was caught up in a five-mile tailback in exactly the same spot as her boss on his first mad dash to the palace four weeks earlier. She sat fuming, half her mind on the reception she could expect, and half on her conversation with Moulay Vella. It wasn't difficult to understand why a small island wanted independence. His premise was totally justifiable, but the idea of hidden assets was hard to believe. An island, he'd said, as rich in antiquities as Rhodes, with enough hidden treasure to revitalise the island and provide much-needed facilities for a proud people. He'd stopped short of identifying the nature of the treasure . . . one bottle more . . . she should have insisted . . . then she too could have shared the secret. Or was he a romancer? A dreamer?

Dwight Jackson finished his morning surgery, sent his receptionist home, made himself a couple of sandwiches, and settled down, thankful to be on his own. He'd been beset with friends and relations all wanting to look after him when all he needed was peace. He'd only taken one bite when he heard the fax working. Couldn't be anything important, he'd finish his lunch first. Half an hour later he sat at his desk in the surgery looking long and hard at the photograph of Moulay Vella. Difficult to tell . . . could be . . . could quite easily be, but there was a niggling doubt. He closed his eyes and sat back in an attempt to recall events of that afternoon, events he'd been trying to forget. First Judy Devereaux's scream, followed by pandemonium as he pushed his way through the crowd, then the dead blonde-haired woman . . . still warm. He remembered how he and Marilyn de Grey had broken the fall of another blonde-haired warder as she fainted, and not long after he began his search for Sarah, who always liked doing her own thing, but she wasn't in the maze, he'd waited half an hour, neither was she in the refurbished Tudor kitchens. Eventually he made his way along the Haunted Gallery, thought he caught a glimpse of Sarah entering the Royal Pew. Followed her in, stood for a moment gazing down on a gloriously restored Tudor Chapel. He remembered seeing the warder and the Japanese party before sitting on a bench in the Long Gallery facing the entrance to the Royal Pew. He was back there again seeing everything clearly. First the family with two children totally out of control who ran the length of the gallery, then a bearded man studying an official guidebook who was followed by that strange woman in a long, hooded robe. She was dressed like a Tudor, carrying spinning-thread and muttering to herself, though he didn't hear a word she said. As she passed the entrance to the Royal Pew a man emerged . . . ran straight into her . . . at which point she vanished. Couldn't have done, he told himself, it's my memory playing tricks. He opened his eyes, took another look at the facsimile of Moulay Vella, and nodded his head. 'Yes, Sarah, that's him.'

At 9.55 the Administrator followed the Head of Security into the Incident Room. Colonel Wishart was puzzled. Why had Sir Elwyn performed a complete volte-face, content now to leave Byrd on the case? He was curious too to learn how this unorthodox policeman was hoping to solve murders with so few leads and such a paucity of clues. Byrd and Mozart were standing over the fax arguing as the two men entered. The Superintendent looked distinctly uptight, and the Inspector his usual lugubrious self.

Sergeant Mayhew ran all the way from the car park to the outer door before composing herself and walking up the stairs and along the corridor. As she opened the door she saw him looking at his watch.

'Glad you've been able to join us, Sergeant,' he said with steel in his voice.

'You did say ten o'clock, sir, didn't you?'

He didn't answer. She sat down, her heart still pumping like a metronome gone berserk.

The meeting began on the dot. WPC Shaw served coffee then sat between Mozart and Mayhew, to take notes.

James Byrd decided not to complicate the issue by giving them the whole picture. There were still issues better kept to himself.

'We all are aware,' he said quietly, 'that two men and a woman, we now know to be Maltese, and possibly the chairman of Olio are involved in three deaths here in the palace. We also know that the first two murders were coincidental, unplanned. The same can't be said for the third which was meticulously engineered enabling the murderers to be miles away from the scene of the crime when death occurred.'

He looked down at the facsimiles in front of him. 'We've just had confirmation that fingerprints on Burgess's glass match those on the document. Confirmation too that those on Vella's glass, used at the wake, match the dabs on a bottle Mayhew found in the bathroom at the Old Rectory. Dr Stormont, who suffered from diabetes, took the tablets daily. Moulay Vella, who we now know was the window cleaner put six tablets containing hematoporphyrin into a bottle containing Tolbutamide. This is the first time in my experience I've come across this horrific method where so many can stand by and watch a man in his dying throes.'

'Why,' asked Tom Abrams, 'didn't Dr Stormont die at home or in his car? Isn't there too great a time lag between Vella placing the tablets in the bottle and Stormont's death?'

'Not if, as I believe, the bottle was well shaken causing the slightly heavier pills to go to the bottom. Peter Stormont, you see, was absent minded, forgot everyday things . . . his keys . . . his appointments . . . taking his medicine . . . so he kept a small bottle in his pocket which was filled from a larger one in the bathroom. Hence the shaking. But we've still no idea when he took the poison because it was a dull wet day when the bandsmen arrived at the palace, and hematoporphyrin is only activated by bright light.'

'Good Lord,' said Mayhew sotto voce.

'What is it, Sergeant?'

'He swallowed some tablets when we were still on the coach . . . just after we'd driven through the Lion Gate.'

'That fits, but it's a pity you didn't say so before.'

'Could have been an asp—'

Colonel Wishart interrupted, eager to get to the root of the matter.

'Forgive me for being dense, Mr Byrd, but if, as you say, this is the first murder in your experience where hema-whatever-it-is has been used, where could it have been purchased, and how did the murderer discover its properties?'

Mozart smiled to himself. Get out of that one.

From the bottom of the pile of papers in front of him the Superintendent extracted a leaflet covered in plastic. 'This article was at one time in Vella's office.'

Mayhew and Mozart looked at each other aghast, fully understanding what their boss had been doing.

Byrd got the vibes, knew exactly what they were thinking.

'It's a leaflet distributed to thousands of Open Collegiate students studying photosynthesis which tells us all we need to know about an experiment carried out in 1912 by a Dr Meyer Betz on himself. He took an infinitesimal dose of hematoporphyrin which produced horrendous swelling on his face, neck and hands, as you can see from this illustration.'

Tom Abrams glanced at it and passed it round. Nothing like as bad as Dr Stormont, but bad enough.

'Betz,' continued Byrd, 'didn't die, he remained sensitive to light for two months and it took another three to desensitise him completely.'

'Presumably you found this in Vella's office at the Francis Bacon Lab,' said Mozart, sailing near the wind.

'Inspector, if we'd gone for a search warrant I'm damned sure that anything of import would've been shredded.'

'Couldn't have concocted it himself. It needs a different type of chemist . . . a pharmacist?'

'Exactly. All he did was contact his brother in Malta who is a chemist. A fine singer too according to Professor Berkeley.'

Abrams gave a guffaw. 'Don't say you've got him at it again? Hope he's getting paid for his services.'

Byrd doodled on the papers in front of him. 'I think we'll leave the Commissioner to sort that out.'

Mayhew again caught the Inspector's eye. He was angry, had only been given half the story. She knew the feeling.

'This brother,' rasped Mozart, 'has a wife or girlfriend, who presumably came over with him on a short break four weeks ago?'

'Yes.'

'So why don't we pick them all up?'

'Two reasons. Malta's not in our jurisdiction, and we don't have sufficient proof to demand extradition. We need to know more, and now Sergeant Mayhew has got her breath back, she'll be able to fill us in, give us some background. She did, after all, have dinner with Vella last night.'

'All expenses paid?' asked Wolfgang maliciously,

She smiled at him. 'Of course.'

'Get on with it, Sergeant.' Her boss, she was pleased to note, was distinctly edgy.

'He's a fanatic. Talks of nothing but his island, and his country, and his people, who he admits, are happy-go-lucky, easygoing and satisfied with their lot. But reading between the lines, I believe there's a strong faction wanting total economic independence. Once Britain was out, Libya was in, offering all kinds of aid, and you know what that means. Vella and his cabal don't want Libyan money or anyone else's money, they believe they can achieve economic freedom by utilising their hidden treasure, about which he wouldn't be drawn. It can't be gold . . . but I just wonder . . .'

'Yes, Sergeant?'

'Oil, sir, or possibly gas?'

'Go on.'

'Oil would obviously attract Olio, and Burgess rang from Malta on the day that Pete died.'

Mozart smirked. At least Charlie knew that much.

'Oil is the answer,' said Byrd pleased with Georgina's deductions. 'The Professor managed a few words with a geophysicist. There are oil and gas deposits in the area south of Gozo, but there's no confirmation yet that the field is sizable enough to justify massive funding.'

'What,' asked Abrams, 'has oil to do with Dr Stormont's death?'

'Everything. He spent years working on solar power for industry, and almost as a sideline began playing around with a solar car. He came up with a formula for an inexpensive car, healthier for us all.'

'And by doing so,' said the Colonel, 'could put oil companies out of business, and Vella's dreams would never materialise.'

'And shares in Olio would drop to an all time low,' said Mozart softly.

'So,' said the Colonel pursuing his train of thought,

'Burgess would also have good reason to assist in the demise of his best friend?'

'His dabs on the document aren't enough. I have to be certain, but there is a way . . .'

'And what about the brother in Malta? Won't you need an extradition order?'

'First of all let's deal with Moulay Vella . . . Mayhew must have another night out on the town.' He noticed her eyes flash and jaw tighten. 'She can let drop that Dr Stormont's plans are here at Hampton Court Palace in his mother's safe. Vella will go for it which will enable us to arrest him for burglary and trespass.'

'But you can't do that,' said the Colonel utterly appalled. 'It's unethical and putting Lady Stormont at risk.'

'She's not lacking in courage, Colonel, and has readily agreed to the scheme providing a distant cousin stays with her for a few days.'

Before Anthony Wishart could object, the Superintendent turned to Mozart.

'Inspector, I've offered your services. You will take on the role of Lady Stormont's distant relation, and sleep in the room next to the study.'

They all looked at Mozart as a variety of expressions flickered across his face. Surprise, disbelief, puzzlement, amusement, and then acceptance.

'Lady S will be quite safe. She'll keep her bedroom door locked at night. It's self-contained, with a telephone, and en suite facilities. A camera will be installed in the study today and when Vella attempts to steal an envelope containing children's drawings the camera will catch him in the act, and then, Inspector, you can arrest him. There will, of course, be two men on the outside making sure he doesn't make a break for it.'

'Yes, sir,' said Mozart happily.

'Anything you want me to do?' asked Abrams.

'Let me know as soon as Vella's on site because I want

Mayhew and Quinney to case his flat in Thorncliffe Road. The Sergeant is quite excellent with locks, he'd have made a fine peterman.'

'What will we be looking for, sir?'

'Any correspondence that links Vella directly with Burgess. It may be our only chance because I guarantee that as soon as Matthew Vella hears his brother's been arrested he'll be here on the next plane to clear the flat.'

Tom Abrams chortled. 'And you will hold him on a customs irregularity.'

Byrd had the grace to laugh. How did you guess? But it will short circuit the procedure of getting him out of Malta. A *fait accompli.*'

Wishart nodded, knowing now why this unorthodox man produced results.

Wolfgang sat there daydreaming. To stay in a Grace and Favour apartment, to stay as a guest where princes had been fêted! What a story to tell his father. He'd almost forgiven the Super for his strange and unexpected methods.

They all looked towards the fax as it began churning out another message. WPC Shaw was on her feet and waiting for a longish message from Dr Dwight Jackson in the States.

James Byrd took it without a 'thank you' but Shaw was rewarded with a smile when he noticed the place of origin. Just what the doctor ordered. He read it through slowly.

'Here gentlemen,' he said brandishing the fax, 'is the last nail in Vella's long overdue coffin. The doctor clearly remembers seeing him rush out of the Royal Pew, bump into a woman dressed in a hooded robe carrying strands of wool or thread, and make his way towards the Queen's Staircase.'

'What!' yelled Tom Abrams and the Colonel in unison.

'Sibell Penn's working overtime,' said Tom.

'Who's Sibell Penn?'

'Our most celebrated and documented ghost,' said the Colonel. 'She nursed Princess Elizabeth through smallpox but caught the disease herself and died shortly afterwards.'

'When did she first materialise?'

'In 1829, I think, when the church in Hampton where she was buried was desecrated and her remains scattered. Shortly afterwards the sound of someone spinning thread was heard in the south-west wing of the palace. The wall was broken down and a hitherto unknown room was discovered in which they found an ancient spinning wheel. It's always been assumed that she returned to the room she occupied during Henry VIII's reign after her remains were disturbed.'

'Do these manifestations coincide with a death in the palace?'

'No . . . I don't think so . . . you're thinking, perhaps, she appeared at the moment Sarah Jackson died?'

'It's a thought.'

'Something,' mused Tom, 'that we should check.'

Mayhew arrived back at her flat in Kidlington planning how she could accidently bump into Vella. Did he have lunch in the lab canteen or had he a favourite eating place? Finally she decided to do nothing, to trust her instinct which rarely let her down, an inherent gift from her Gaelic forbears. When she'd had a shower and slipped into a loose kaftan she switched on the answerphone which delivered an arrogant message: 'Georgina, meet me for dinner at the Randolph tomorrow at 7.30. Coffee afterwards at my place.' She was livid, his intentions were loud and clear, but somehow between the soup and the savoury she'd sort him out.

He was on his best behaviour, so too was Georgina, but this time she'd very little make-up on and was wearing her plain blue dress. She felt slightly dirty, dishonest, leading him up the garden path, until she reminded herself he was a murderer. An eye for an eye, she thought savagely.

Over the excellent pheasant which they washed down with a 1985 Châteauneuf du Pape she nattered on about her sketches of the church, and Jane's problems giving a graphic description of a window cleaner who'd actually climbed into the bathroom. She talked about Jane's fears and why Pete's plans were now in his mother's safe at Hampton Court Palace. When she imparted this snippet of information she looked him straight in the eyes, but he gave nothing away, his face deadpan and his dark eyes slightly glazed, but she didn't miss the slight tautening of his hands as he gripped his knife and fork more tightly, nor the way he cut his pheasant with careful precision. Mission accomplished, she thought happily.

Vella, too, was happy. He'd plenty to celebrate . . . shouldn't be too difficult to get his hands on the plans.

'We'll go to town,' he said joyfully, 'we'll have a bottle of Monbazillac with the dessert.'

On your head be it, she thought, after choosing a chocolate mousse from the sweet trolley. It was delicious but she bided her time . . . not too soon . . . start on the cheese first. Halfway through the ripe, mouth-watering Stilton she gasped, and clasped her head with both hands.

'What's the matter, Georgina?'

'I'm sorry, Moulay, I really am, but I'm an idiot . . . do you know what I've done?'

He shook his head.

'I've eaten chocolate, a damn silly thing to do because it nearly always gives me migraine . . . I just didn't think . . .'

Only then did she see any emotion. A flash of anger quickly dispelled by an assumed mask of concern.

Georgina rang her boss at home.

'Byrd,' he barked.

'Operation completed, sir.'

'Good. Tomorrow, Sergeant, I want you in Tooting at 6.30 in the morning. Get Simpson out of bed, and ask him the following questions.'

'Just as well I didn't sample the Monbazillac.'

'What's that?'

'Nothing, sir, nothing.'

Moulay Vella sat in his flat at 15A Thorncliffe Road thinking about the plans he'd been so desperately seeking. Fortuitous to learn of their whereabouts in such a roundabout way. Georgina rewarding him with one hand and taking away with the other! Stupid, she'd been, and greedy not able to control her childhood lust, just like a woman. He'd read about chocolate causing headaches and producing hyperactivity in young children, but could four or five spoonfuls of mousse produce a devastating migraine and how did she manage to drive home?

A pity, he wanted to know the woman, not just her body, her mind too. There was a quality which had intrigued him from the very first moment, hidden strengths in an attractive divorcee, not short of cash and totally independent, who idled away her time producing rather amateurish sketches. They were travelling in different directions. Deep down he knew there'd never be another chance . . . but at least she'd told him what he wanted to know. Suddenly he stiffened. All that girlish chat throughout the meal didn't fit the image . . . she wasn't the type. Got it! What a fool I've been. She's setting me up. Despite the warm night he shivered, wondering who she was working for, how much she knew, how much they knew? Nothing . . . but he couldn't convince himself. There'd been no developments on the case for a month, but surely if they'd made a breakthrough something would have leaked. He decided to check, get down to the health club tomorrow, make sure.

Sergeant Mayhew, smartly dressed in a pale green trouser suit, pressed the bell alongside the name of Simmons. It was 6.28. She gave them until 6.30 before pressing again, longer this time and with intent.

An irate voice shouting, 'Who the hell is that?' made her smile. That's exactly what she'd have said in the circumstances.

'Police, Mr Simmons. I need to speak to you.'

'Why? Has something happened to Mother?'

'No, sir.'

'What then?'

'We can't talk like this, sir. I have to see you.'

There was a long silence. He knew the voice – had to put a face to it – gradually a picture emerged, the church and the pub, and a woman crossing the road.

'Come on up,' he said at last. 'We're on the first floor.'

Sally Simmons opened the door. 'You'd better come in and wait. My husband's getting dressed.'

'Thank you.'

'Must be serious disturbing us at this hour?'

'Difficult to say, Mrs Simmons, until I've talked to your husband.'

'Take a pew in the lounge, and I'll make some coffee.'

Georgina sank down into a Victorian sofa which had seen better days. The room was tastefully but not extravagantly furnished. New carpets but old furniture. He wasn't in the money, she felt sure of that. Simmons, looking very bad tempered and unshaven, carried in a tray and dumped it on the occasional table beside his unwelcome visitor.

'Help yourself.' He didn't even give her time to thank him. 'Now what's all this about, and hadn't you better show me your warrant?'

She took her time, let him see that she wasn't going to

be hustled. He peered at it . . . looked at the photograph and then back at the subject.

'About time you had another one taken.'

'Mr Simmons, there's no need to get personal about this. I'm on a job, sent here to interview you, so why don't we get on with it?'

'OK. Get on with it, though I can't imagine why the police are interested in me.'

'You drive for Sir Hubert Morrissey, don't you?'

'Yeh.'

'Is that your only job?'

'Yeh.'

'Have you ever driven Sir Hubert to Hampton Court Palace?'

'Yeh.'

'Did you know Dr Stormont?'

'Only by sight.'

'And Paul Burgess, know him?'

'No.'

'How about Moulay Vella?'

'Yeh, yeh, I know him.'

'Do you have business dealings with him?'

'No,' he said angrily. 'I've already told you I do one job. No moonlighting.'

'How often do you see Vella, and where?'

'Once a week at the health club in Tottenham Court Road when he comes up to town.'

'You talk to him, do you?'

'Occasionly in the sauna after training.'

'Does he ask you about your job?'

'Sometimes, though a chauffeur's day can be described in two seconds. Drive and wait.'

Georgina laughed. 'I'm sure there's more to it than that.'

'Why don't you come clean, Sergeant? Moulay's up to something, isn't he?'

'Yes. Perhaps you can tell me,' she asked swiftly trying to catch him off balance, 'how Vella knew that Dr Stormont and Sir Hubert met at Hampton Court?'

'If you're bloody suggesting I told him, you've got it all wrong.'

Dickybird's got it all wrong, thought Georgina, this man's on the level.

'But . . . half a minute . . .' he sat down, closed his eyes. 'Yes, we talked once, we certainly did, didn't we, about what we'd had for lunch, about keeping our weight under control, you understand. I remember telling him I often enjoyed my picnic lunch in the Rolls in a centuries-old environment and . . . oh my God . . . I've been bloody stupid. Careless too.'

'Don't worry, Mr Simmons, it wasn't your fault.'

'It's tied up, isn't it, with those deaths at Hampton Court? I'm an idiot, never thought anything about it, and I've spent my life keeping my mouth shut, been in that sort of job.'

'I know, but you can make amends.'

'How?'

'Tomorrow's Thursday. Will you be at the club?' He nodded. 'If Vella's there give me a call on this number.' She handed him a card. 'Act normally, don't alert him. And thanks, Mr Simmons, thanks.'

'Now you're here you might as well have breakfast.'

'Can I take a raincheck? I've another urgent call to make.'

'Any time, Sergeant, any time except half past six in the morning!'

Mayhew left Veronica Road at 7.15, determined to be in Oxford by 9.30. She'd take a leaf out of Dickybird's book, had to because she'd blotted her copybook, hadn't completed the mission, hadn't returned to Vella's flat and played out the charade. He was too intelligent not to question why she'd fed him the information, then suffered a migraine which struck like lightning. Such indisposition saved her from Vella's advances but didn't protect her from the wrath of Superintendent Byrd. He would have expected her to dream up a better escape route. She should have gone to the flat, made herself physically sick . . . easy enough, that's what she should have done.

She reached the outskirts of Oxford by 9.30 as planned, parked the car at the Little Chef, made a phone call, checked with Maureen Kennedy that Moulay would be tied up at work for the rest of the morning, swallowed a piping-hot coffee and made her way to Thorncliffe Road. The job would have been easier with Sergeant Quinney at her side, but she couldn't get him in *shtook* if this didn't work.

Permit parking for residents took up every available space so she drove round the block again and parked outside the shops in the Banbury Road and ran back to 15A. As she'd driven by the first time she'd noticed the door of 15 was open and two women were gossiping outside number 9, too intent on discussing the merits of roses to notice a stranger slip into the house. Inside the hall were two doors, 15A to the right. It was firmly locked, but with a yale which gave way beneath the pressure of her Access card. She closed the door and crept up the stairs, the bathroom and kitchen doors were open, but the two facing her at the top of the stairs were shut. She stood listening for several minutes before daring to enter the front room. It was curiously clinical, plain white emulsioned walls, modern furniture, no pictures, no books, no desk, no cupboard, no drawers. She hoped the bedroom had more to offer. As she'd expected, a double bed, but much more interesting was the large old-fashioned bureau with a concertina'd sliding lid standing in front of the window. She turned the key and slid it open. It was immaculately tidy, easy to leave things as they were. Systematically she read through weekly letters from his mother which told her nothing, occasional letters from his brother, and birthday greetings from his sister. As she was sifting through his bills the front door banged. 'Oh no,' she whispered, as she quickly closed the desk and crawled under the bed. Her damned perfume was a giveaway, another blunder. From the room below she could hear movement and a woman talking to someone, but her companion never replied. It soon became clear that the someone was her cat. She breathed a sigh of relief and settled down again to search through the desk. There was nothing in the drawers, in the pigeonholes, or on top of the desk. Lastly, before leaving, she flicked open the desk blotter and therein lay the treasure trove. She wanted to shout for joy, but remembered the lady and the cat. It was more than she deserved. A brief note from Paul Burgess asking the Vella brothers to meet him at Hampton Court Palace a week on Sunday, where he'd be staying with Lady Stormont. She copied it, not leaving out a single comma.

As Stephanie sleepily turned over she realised she was alone. What was the matter with him? For several nights now he'd hardly slept; she knew he was sitting in the easy chair brooding.

'Why don't you talk about it?' she asked softly.

'Sorry, darling, didn't mean to wake you.'

'You know your trouble, James?'

'Yes, but you'll never change me.'

'One day you'll have to share the burden, talk things over with your colleagues. Talking things over helps to clarify ideas.'

'It's the last ten per cent . . . it defies discussion. Ninety per cent is crystal clear, we've enough evidence to charge the Vella brothers, but I need incontrovertible evidence connecting them to Burgess.'

'You'll never do that by spending the night in a Lloyd Loom chair.'

'I'd half made up my mind to bring him in.'

'Didn't you say he lives in Abingdon? It's not so far.'

Her thoughts were loud and clear.

'You're right, I'll get down there now . . . call on him before breakfast, catch him with his pants down.'

She laughed, 'Literally or metaphorically, darling?'

He reached Abingdon as Mayhew left Tooting on a misty morning which heralded another sweltering day in the upper seventies. The palatial house abutted the river with a narrowboat moored at the end of the garden. Once such a happy playing ground for Stephen and Sandra, but what now? Would their godfather carry out his duties, his promise to look after their welfare or was that window-dressing?

As he parked the car in the forecourt he saw Burgess watching him from an upstairs window. By the time he reached the front door it was open.

'Come in, Superintendent, I've been expecting you.'

James Byrd, who thought he was springing the surprises, was slightly taken aback.

'Anthea, my wife, is spending a few days with her mother in Richmond. Gives me time to concentrate my mind on winding up one of our recent explorations which shows no promise. But, Mr Byrd, you haven't come to discuss my family life, you've come to talk business. I suggest we chat over a frugal breakfast. Cereal, toast and coffee, that do you?'

'Yes, thanks, do very nicely.'

Burgess finished off his muesli at speed, poured a second cup of coffee for them both and then astounded the policeman. 'You're here, of course, about the document I was enveigled into presenting to Peter, which he quite sensibly refused to sign. I was angry at the time, not so much because Pete would have nothing to do with it, but angry because the syndicate had spent weeks putting the proposition on paper. They wasted their time, the Government's time, and my time which unfortunately culminated in verbal sparring with Peter. This document is dynamite.'

'I know, Mr Burgess, I have the original copy.'

'Good God, I looked everywhere. Where did you find it?'

'Sergeant Mayhew was on her way to Sarum when she accidently found it in her hands.'

'You mean Georgina is a policewoman?'

'Yes.'

'If I'd known that I wouldn't have worried about Jane's safety.'

'Tell me about this document, Mr Burgess.'

Half an hour later James Byrd was a wiser man, versed in how cartels and governments worked when big money was at stake. Knew exactly why Sir Hubert had had misgivings. A certain cabal interested in the profits from oil, and recognising no frontiers, had embraced men in Government circles both in Britain and the Middle East, as well as countries bordering the North Sea. They'd formed a syndicate to prevent the development of Stormont's inexpensive solar car. Offered him a fortune which he turned down believing his children and his grandchildren should inherit a greener world.

'I went home that day, Mr Byrd, ashamed that I'd allowed Olio to become enmeshed in a scheme propounded by my so-called friends in Government. It was made clear to me that Britain desperately needs oil currency, far more important it seems than worrying about poisoning the population.'

'Britain's not the only country, Mr Burgess. How about the undiscovered wealth in the Mediterranean . . . south of Gozo, for instance?'

'Oh, you know about that, do you? Well, it's off as far as Olio's concerned. We're pulling out. A perfectly legitimate excuse . . . the field isn't large enough, and when that withdrawal is complete I'm stepping down as chairman of Olio and carrying on with Peter's experiment.'

'That's why you took the red car.'

'Yes. And you have the yellow one, do you not?'

Byrd frowned, thinking how wrong he'd been, but he hadn't reached the end yet . . . there was an undercurrent . . . a certain caution in the way the case had been presented.

As if in answer to his thoughts Burgess half smiled. 'He was my star pupil, no one I've ever met has had such talent in so many fields. I loved that man, Mr Byrd, as if he were my own son; his work will not be wasted.'

'His plans,' said Byrd after considerable thought, 'are in the bank.'

'Yes, he told me over the phone two days before his death, but I forgot to ask him what he'd done with the document. I wanted to destroy it before an unscrupulous operator sold it to the Sunday newspapers.'

On his way to Hampton Court Palace he realised his own shortcomings had been exacerbated by lack of sleep. Why couldn't he share the load? Why did he always allow his instincts and his hunches to have sway instead of using cold reason and logic? He had a hunch now . . . leading to an unbelievable scenario . . . but it was the stuff Hitchcock films were made of, not the real world. On the other hand sometimes his hunches worked where all else failed . . .

Mayhew was waiting for him. She looked happy, the green get-up suited her. He was right about Simmons, he had let slip the Minister's itinerary, not with malice aforethought, but a slight lapse for which he'd now make amends. He was annoyed with Mayhew for casing Vella's flat on her own. Putting her job at risk was bloody stupid for a woman with her ability. They might ignore a man's breach of the rules, but never a woman's. An act like that could have remained on her record never to be wiped off, but he had to admit she was quite a character. A character who'd returned to base with the goodies. He read and reread the note. What the hell was Burgess up to now? Curiously it fitted in with his scenario, but it wouldn't happen that way, it couldn't. The deal with the Maltese was over, Olio was getting out, so why the meeting?'

Tom Abrams greeted him with the good news that the media, much to Colonel Wishart's relief, was off their backs. For three whole days not a murmur from the press or a peep from TV.

Inspector Mozart had enjoyed his three days living it up in Lady Stormont's apartment, but was glad to get back to his new toy, now part of his life. Recent notes from Byrd and Mayhew kept him busy for a few hours, and when he'd got the picture he was over the moon. He took a guess at what might happen, it could so easily occur from the way Charlie had spelt things out . . . but Dickybird had said nothing, Dickybird wouldn't let it happen, would he?

In mid morning Lawrence Berkeley rang from Gatwick with another snippet of news. He'd travelled on the same plane as Olio's geophysicist who'd let drop, while they were waiting to board, that there was oil, plenty of it, but the chairman had decided not to proceed.

Simmons continued methodically with his press-ups, and stretching, 45, 46, 47, 48, 49, 50. As he turned over to extend his legs and arms he was aware that Vella, who was working on the weights, was looking in his direction. He missed the weightlifting, he'd done it for years when he was with the SAS, but since the accident it was out, would have done irreparable damage. Stretching, swimming, walking and badminton had helped him on the way to recovery, and were now the only pursuits in which he dabbled.

Vella had given up and was walking his way.

'Hi there, Michael, see you in the sauna.'

What's he after now, wondered the man lying flat on a gym mat counting up to fifty? At the end of his fifth lot of press-ups he made no move, lay there thinking, let the bugger sweat it out in the sauna for ten minutes, he'd cool off first and enjoy a leisurely swim.

As he ambled into the sauna, Vella, who'd spread himself, moved over to make room for him.

'Everything OK, Mike?'

'Yeh, everything.'

'Still driving your VIP around?'

'Yeh.' Not wasting much time, thought Simmons, in getting to the point.

'Weren't you at Hampton Court Palace with him the day of the murders?'

'Murders!'

'Yes, those two women.'

'Yeh, I guess I was, but I swear I didn't do it.'

Moulay's artificial laugh echoed round the cubicle. 'If you didn't do it, who did, that's the sixty-four dollar question.'

Simmons concentrated on drying his ears.

'Odd, isn't it, how the whole thing's quietened down.'

'What do you expect from that dimwitted policeman who's in charge of the case?'

'I wouldn't have said he was dim, I met him, you know, at Dr Stormont's funeral.'

'A difficult case,' murmured Simmons so softly that Vella had to lean right over him to hear. 'Too many people around, motiveless killings, can't expect the police to turn water into wine, you know.'

Vella didn't follow his gist, but he laughed because he felt safer, although he still couldn't fathom why Georgina had so readily told him where the plans were secreted. He'd make no attempt to break in, he'd wait until the meeting with Burgess who'd be staying there. The gods favoured him, so why chance his arm?

Simmons felt Vella relax, the tension ooze away, and knew that if he looked into the man's eyes they'd be brighter.

He'd call that gorgeous Sergeant with the sexy voice before he returned home.

No fun those damned answerphones. All he got was an impersonal voice telling him to wait for the tone, then when he'd cleared his throat the waves recorded his version of thirty minutes in a West End sauna.

9

Lady Stormont felt a little lost without Mozart around. An odd man, he'd hardly said a word the first day, just sat gazing happily at the pictures, the furniture. It was only when they were in the kitchen, she washing the dishes and he wiping them, that they developed a burgeoning rapport. His massive hands fondled the Coalport china lovingly, drying each piece carefully before placing it in the kitchen cabinet.

'Indian Tree,' he murmured, 'my mother would have loved it, she always fancied being a potter.'

After that there was no stopping him. He talked as he'd never talked before. She became totally immersed in another way of life, a life she couldn't have imagined, stranger than any fictional tale, never dreaming that three people could live a lifetime together without mentioning their love, their joy or their sorrow. Mozart failed to realise Lady Stormont had become his willing mother–confessor releasing tensions he'd never recognised, neither did he realise she was tiring from the strain of listening and concentrating for several hours. She was a person who lived within herself who since her husband's death had come to terms with loneliness, but she did nothing to discourage her guest, letting him talk the hours away. She was both sorry and relieved to see him go, but two days later when she heard a tentative knock she rushed to the door hoping he'd returned.

She was utterly dumbfounded to find Paul Burgess standing there. They stared at each other for some seconds, they could have been strangers.

'You'd better come in,' she said at last. He followed her into the sitting room. 'Why've you come?'

'To talk about Peter . . . about his work . . . what I hope to do.'

'You'd better sit down, then.'

Two hours later Byrd caught a glimpse of them walking round the grounds looking at the final preparations for the flower show beginning on the morrow. They stood for an age gazing at the staging which had been built over the Long Water to provide a local chamber orchestra with plenty of space.

'Peter,' she said, 'would have enjoyed all this, a proper stage for the band, and a bigger audience than he had . . .'

Paul took her hand, 'Try not to think about it. Remember, only, that his work will go on.'

'I misjudged you Paul, I'm sorry.

'You didn't. This is my road to Damascus.'

WPC Shaw, who'd been ordered to wear a summer dress and a headscarf, was seemingly admiring the sweet-scented roses adjacent to the car park when a white Cavalier hatchback arrived. The two young men thought themselves lucky as the driver angled the car into the last remaining space. Shaw, who'd dreamed of transferring to the CID, followed her instructions to the letter.

'White Cavalier has parked. Suspects are walking my way.'

She bent down to smell the roses as they strolled past her, then she followed the two men who'd arrived back at the scene of their crime.

Abrams, Mayhew and Mozart all heard the cryptic message, so too did James Byrd, out of sight, in the ticket office situated in the Barrack Block a stone's throw from the Trophy Gate, where until the end of the First World War horses had been stabled and soldiers lodged. He waited. Instinct told him Burgess would purchase tickets. In the meantime, Tom Abrams, whom the Chairman of Olio didn't know and wouldn't recognise, idled away his time by keeping watch on Lady Stormont's apartment while Mayhew, in a long mousey-coloured wig, dark glasses and a straw hat, stood outside the Chaplain's House keeping her eyes glued on Tilt Yard.

Tom saw Burgess leave the apartment, and heard Lady Stormont wishing him luck. 'Subject leaving now,' he said succinctly.

'Shaw, what's happening out there?' asked the Superintendent.

'They look uneasy, sir, they're deep in conversation walking round the rose garden. I wouldn't be surprised if they leave the car and do a bunk on foot.'

'I've no time for theories, Shaw, just stay with them.'

'Yes, sir.'

Five minutes later Georgina saw Burgess approaching from the south side of the palace. He appeared to be in no hurry as he ambled his way towards the ticket office. Shortly afterwards Byrd heard a deep baritione voice asking for three tickets.

'What's he done, sir?' asked the lady who'd dispensed the ticket, thrilled to be in the action.

'Nothing yet, Mrs Clarke.'

Burgess perched himself on the crenellations alongside the old moat and waited. The policeman on duty was annoyed at his apparent disregard for the ancient stone structure, but daren't move him. He too had been given explicit instructions.

Shaw shouted excitedly that the two men were leaving.

'Keep it down, Constable, they'll hear you.'

'Sorry, sir. They're leaving the rose garden and walking down Tennis Court . . .'

'I've got them,' interrupted Georgina. 'They've seen the subject. They're walking towards him; they're shaking hands; now they seem to be arguing; The subject is insisting on something and they're shaking their heads; they've given in, shrugging their shoulders and going along with it. They're moving towards the Gatehouse; they're going in now, sir.'

Inspector Mozart had his men from the Royal Parks Police in position. Every exit was covered. The brothers could have been arrested the moment they'd arrived but Byrd, whose gut feeling told him Burgess wasn't involved, had to be sure. He had to know about their future plans, might learn details he didn't know about their past activities.

Shaw must keep close, only then could he hear what was being said.

The chairman of Olio led the two brothers through the Great Hall.

'Impressive, isn't it? Been here before, have you?'

'Many years ago,' said Moulay.

'And you, Matthew?'

'Never,' he said brusquely. 'Why don't we cut the historic tour and get down to business . . . discuss our latest proposition?'

'It will keep, we'll chat over lunch.'

'We haven't much time. I must be on the 4.30 plane.'

'Relax, my friend. Heathrow's only down the road. Let me show you some of the wonders of the Tudor Palace. First the Great Watching Chamber.'

WPC Shaw close on their heels followed them through the Horn Room.

'Here in this Chamber, only a month ago,' said Burgess with no inflexion whatsoever, 'a young woman slipped and sprained her ankle, an action which held up visitors for quite a time.'

'What are you getting at?' asked Moulay tersely, stopping in his tracks and looking to his brother for help.

Matthew was distinctly uneasy, knew he shouldn't have

come, but Moulay, as usual, had been persuasive, said he could get his hands on the plans, provided his brother kept tabs on Burgess and Lady Stormont during the opening of the flower show at two o'clock.

'For God's sake, let's get outside in the open, it's stifling in here.'

'I disagree, Matthew, these rooms are always cool. Bear with me a little before we get down to business. You can't possibly return to Malta without seeing some of the glories of Hampton Court.'

WPC Shaw followed them along the Haunted Gallery towards the Royal Pew.

'This is a bloody waste of time,' said Moulay irritably.

'It'll only take a few minutes. Perhaps you were in too much of a hurry last time you were here to appreciate the wondrous roof in the Royal Chapel?'

Matthew grabbed his brother's arm. 'We're not going along with this, are we?' he whispered.

Shaw dithered, not knowing what to do. 'Sir,' she breathed, they're just going into the Royal Pew . . . I'd be a bit obvious . . .'

'You're right. Stay put, take your headscarf off and sit on the bench until they come out.'

Burgess is playing a dangerous game, thought James Byrd, putting himself at risk by trying to extract a confession . . . maybe he should arrest them now? But there were one or two loose ends . . . threads he might unravel . . . safe enough for the moment with two men on duty in the Royal Pew. Burgess with his two unwilling companions stood gazing at the roof of the Chapel. Moulay was sweating . . . couldn't understand what Paul was at . . . never did anything without reason . . . setting them up, was he? For what? Using blackmail to make sure negotiations went Olio's way . . . more money for Olio, less for Malta . . . that was it . . . the man was a crook! Matthew, he noticed, was getting edgy, always likely to lose his cool and do something stupid . . . must calm him down . . . can't say much with these policemen around.

'Mr Burgess,' shouted Matthew angrily, 'let's get to hell out of here, we're wasting time, we're getting nowhere.'

'Quiet please, sir,' said PC Wilkins.

'Bear with me, Matthew, ten minutes, and then we'll get down to brass tacks . . . get down to business.'

Get down to business . . . thought Byrd . . . get down to business. My God, I'm an imbecile . . . I've done it again . . . like the Tower I've given them too much rope . . . should have picked them up in the car park.

'Tom! Mayhew! Get over to the Queen's Apartments, and Mozart stand by at the bottom of the Queen's Staircase. Bring a couple of men with you.'

'What's up, sir?' It was a reflex action, he should have known better.

'Just get there, Mozart.' Now what the hell was going on?

Tom ran up the Queen's Stairs meeting Mayhew who'd sprinted along the Haunted Gallery faster than the unhappy Catherine Howard. They entered the Queen's Guard Chamber together where, through the open doorway, they could see Burgess pointing to the bed where the corpse of Doris Veasey had lain. Byrd by this time had reached the Communications Gallery. He stopped, got his breath back and listened.

'That bed, friends,' said a rich baritone, 'was made for Queen Anne. We have an odd sort of joke in this country, something you may not have come across. If anything's old, or out of date we say Queen Anne's dead. Strange, isn't it, because Queen Anne didn't die here, but an innocent unsuspecting wardress did. A woman who was poisoned with a rare but vitriolic snake venom. It proved so efficacious, Matthew, that I'm surprised you don't sell it over the counter.'

'It was necessary,' snarled Matthew, 'they had to be

silenced, even you must see that.'

'And Stormont's death, was that necessary? You could certainly have taught the Borgias a thing or two. I feel grief for the unfortunate ladies whom I didn't know, but Peter was my friend.'

'Mine too,' said Moulay, 'but he was going to destroy us, deprive us of our heritage, don't you understand?'

'Yes, I understand perfectly.'

'Nothing must stand in our way. It's a case of life and death. Survival of my people.'

'No thought for your victims? No compassion?'

'Nothing is ever achieved without sacrifice, so let's get talking.'

'OK, but first of all you must see Wolsey's Closet, a perfect example of Tudor decor, colourful, rich.'

Byrd was nearest, he ran into the Closet and secreted himself in a small alcove.

Burgess led the Vella brothers back through the Queen's Guard Chamber where Tom and Georgina quickly mingled with a group whose lecturer was extolling the artistry of Christopher Wren.

As Moulay passed the group he was wondering how he and his brother could deal with Burgess who'd suddenly changed from a benefactor into a monster. He'd no eyes for the woman in a mousey wig nor was he aware of WPC Shaw who'd trailed them from the moment they'd arrived.

To Byrd the footfalls of the three men sounded like an army marching, but through the noise he managed to hear Burgess.

'There are two excellent murals in Wolsey's private closet which I'm sure, Moulay, you'll appreciate.'

'Tom,' whispered Byrd, 'you still with them?'

'Yes.'

'Stand outside the Closet, but stay close.'

Paul Burgess ushered his guests into the small room,

and planting himself behind them, stood in the doorway his bulk filling the space.

'Aren't these two murals superb, gentlemen?'

Moulay, thinking he'd worked out the rationale behind Burgess's actions, was prepared to pay lip service.

'Yes, Paul, superb.'

'I haven't time for all this culture,' growled Matthew. 'I've a plane to catch.'

Paul ignored him. 'Take a close look at *The Last Supper*, painted over an earlier work. Brings to mind, doesn't it, two characteristics, loyalty and betrayal? Betrayal for a price.'

Sergeant Mayhew held her breath waiting for an answer . . . but the brothers were silent, and their accuser continued relentlessly.

'Dr Stormont, like Christ, trusted the men who worked with him. He trusted you, Moulay.'

There was another long silence . . . Mayhew gazed at Abrams. *Not yet*, he was mouthing.

Mozart, listening, at the bottom of the Queen's Staircase was distinctly uneasy. He felt the tension, knew something would give, so with his men he quietly mounted the stairs.

'Now,' said Burgess, breaking the silence, 'take a look at *The Scourging*, a mural which shows Christ punishing the sinners.'

He looked coldly at the two men who, for the first time, were totally unnerved.

'Peter's not here to demand retribution,' he said quietly, 'but I am.'

The brothers said nothing. They looked at the murals . . . then at each other . . . their moment of truth . . . and they were powerless . . . they'd come unprepared . . . no syringe . . . no poison.

Suddenly there was a shout from Moulay. 'No, you can't.'

Byrd couldn't see the gun in Paul's hand, but he, like Tom and Georgina, heard a click as the safety catch was released. *Hell! I have done it again . . . gone too far.*

Abrams nodded to Mayhew, indicating she was to grab Burgess's left arm. At the same moment as Byrd stepped out of the alcove to face the muzzle of a Biretta, Abrams, with a sudden movement, grasped Burgess's right arm bending it upwards and backwards forcing him to drop the weapon while Matthew made a move towards the revolver, but he was too late, Byrd kicked it into touch, unreachable in the alcove behind him.

'Let's get out of here,' said Moulay, 'that bastard was trying to kill us.'

The would-be assassin stood there, with a slight smile on his face, rubbing his bruised right arm, thankful it wasn't broken.

'Kill you? That's what I would like to have done, but you've confessed. You've said enough. I'll let Nemesis take her course.'

'You're bloody joking. We've not admitted anything. It's your word against ours, and who's going to believe the word of an assassin?' snarled Moulay.

'To be an assassin one needs three things,' said Burgess slowly. 'Intent. A gun. And bullets.'

There was a guffaw from Abrams as he dived into the alcove and picked up the Biretta. He broke it open and with a broad grin shoved an unloaded revolver under Moulay's nose before handing it back to its owner.

'Could have been a painful joke, I might have broken your arm.'

'All this,' said Matthew belligerently, 'makes no difference. He used threatening behaviour, and I'll get my solicitor on to it.'

'Rubbish,' said Paul, 'you've admitted everything.'

'We've admitted nothing because there's nothing to admit'

'That's where you're wrong,' said Byrd softly. 'We took

a leaf out of your book, Mr Vella. We've recorded every word. We even acquired a wig, not a long black curly job, but a less noticeable mousey one.'

Georgina, thankful to be rid of it, took off her straw hat and then removed the wig.

'You! yelled Moulay. 'You bitch!'

'Inspector Mozart, are you there?' shouted Byrd.

'Yes, sir.'

'Take over, will you. Arrest these men. Get them down to the station and charge them with three murders and one attempted murder.'

'Attempted murder!' sneered Matthew. 'You make things up as you go along.

'Mr Moulay Vella will also be charged with attempting to murder Dr Stormont as he walked through the wood near his home with his two young children.'

Matthew looked at his brother. 'You idiot, you bloody idiot.'

Wolfgang thought for a moment that he was hearing things. After all these years he was going to make the most important arrest in his entire career. Byrd's voice sounded a long way off.

'You've got everything you need, Inspector, to process the case. Shaw has recorded their confessions, and Charlie can fill you in on everything else.'

'Are you leaving today, sir?'

'My Chief wants to see me at four o'clock . . . leaves me enough time for a cup of coffee in the Incident Room providing Shaw gets her skates on.'

WPC Shaw who could see nothing and hear everything knew her moment of glory was over. Now she was tea-boy again, and tomorrow she'd be in uniform.

'Yes, sir,' she said despondently.

* * *

Colonel Wishart joined Byrd, Abrams, Burgess and Mayhew for coffee. His faith in this extraordinary man totally justified, but the charge of attempted murder was something new.

'How, Mr Bryd, did you turn up this evidence, such a difficult thing to prove on hearsay. No rifle, no bullets.'

'I didn't know . . . had half hoped during Burgess's interrogation that everything would fall into place.'

'It's news to me,' said Paul, 'Pete never mentioned a sharp shooter hidden in the trees.'

'Incidentally,' said Abrams, 'if the Biretta had been loaded would you still have shot using only your right hand?'

'Yes.'

'Much more accurate if you use both, you should try it sometime.'

'Let's forget the weapon for a moment,' said Byrd, 'in case Mr Burgess hasn't yet obtained a licence.

'You've no worries there, I've had one for years, but for a few seconds, I must admit, I scared myself, didn't realise how much I hated them, how much I wanted to kill them, and how easy it would have been.'

Mayhew shivered. All she remembered seeing was her boss facing the gun . . . thinking that at any moment . . . she shook herself . . . it hadn't happened . . . the nightmare had been momentary.

'I've just heard, Mr Byrd,' said the Colonel, 'that you're seeing Sir Charles later this afternoon. Another case, I gather. Any idea where?'

'All I know is I've three days leave. After that, you could say it's a busman's holiday. I'll be spending a couple of days at the Royal Shakespeare Theatre as a member of the audience. What more can a man ask?'

They all looked at him in amazement.

He laughed. 'I can see you're as baffled as I am.'

* * *

The four o'clock meeting with his Chief Constable at Divisional HQ went on far too long. James Byrd was dying to get home. Three days peace in Bletchingdon, nowhere in the world so dear to him. Before leaving Kidlington he rang Stephanie to let her know he'd be home by seven at the latest.

'Open a bottle, Stephie, we'll celebrate the solving of the Hampton Court case, and tomorrow we'll sit in the garden, sun ourselves and discuss our holiday plans.'

'Tomorrow, but tomorrow James I'll . . .' She sounded joyful, elated.

'Go on.'

'Tomorrow, I'll not be here.'

'What do you mean?'

'I'm starting a new job in Oxford with Sprott and Salisbury.'

'But you never mentioned . . .'

'They rang at four o'clock, said they were short staffed.'

'Can't you put it off?'

'No, not now. I can't possibly let them down.'

'You mean I'll be on my own?'

'Yes, James, I'm afraid you will.'